Iridescent Soul

The Story
The Music

M.L Stevens

Copyright © 2001 by M.L Stevens

ISBN 0-7414-0758-2

Published by:

Infinity Publishing.com
519 West Lancaster Avenue
Haverford, PA 19041-1413
Info@buybooksontheweb.com
www.buybooksontheweb.com
Toll-free (877) BUY BOOK
Local Phone (610) 520-2500
Fax (610) 519-0261

Printed in the United States of America

Printed on Recycled Paper

Published October, 2001

What Others Are Saying About
Iridescent Soul

Iridescent Soul has given me great comfort.
Donna Plock - Loveland, Colorado

This was a nice experience—spiritual and passionate and deeply felt.
Larry Gates - Portal Productions, Portal, Arizona

Thank you for this gift. I will treasure it for many years.
Janet Creason - Overland Park, Kansas

THANK YOU for Iridescent Soul. It blew us away!
Linda and Jim Hoskins - Eagan, Minnesota

Wow! What an inspiring story! This was tremendous!
Lea Opitz - Broomfield, Colorado

I have just read your beautiful story about the hummingbird
and I am feeling so overwhelmed by the joy/sadness of it.
I love reading, but only two stories have ever really had
this effect on me—Jonathan Livingston Seagull by Richard Bach,
and The Little Soul And The Sun by Neale Donald Walsch.
I compare your beautiful story with these and thank you
so much for writing it. I feel blessed for having read it.
Lisa Butler - Imagination Songs, Australia

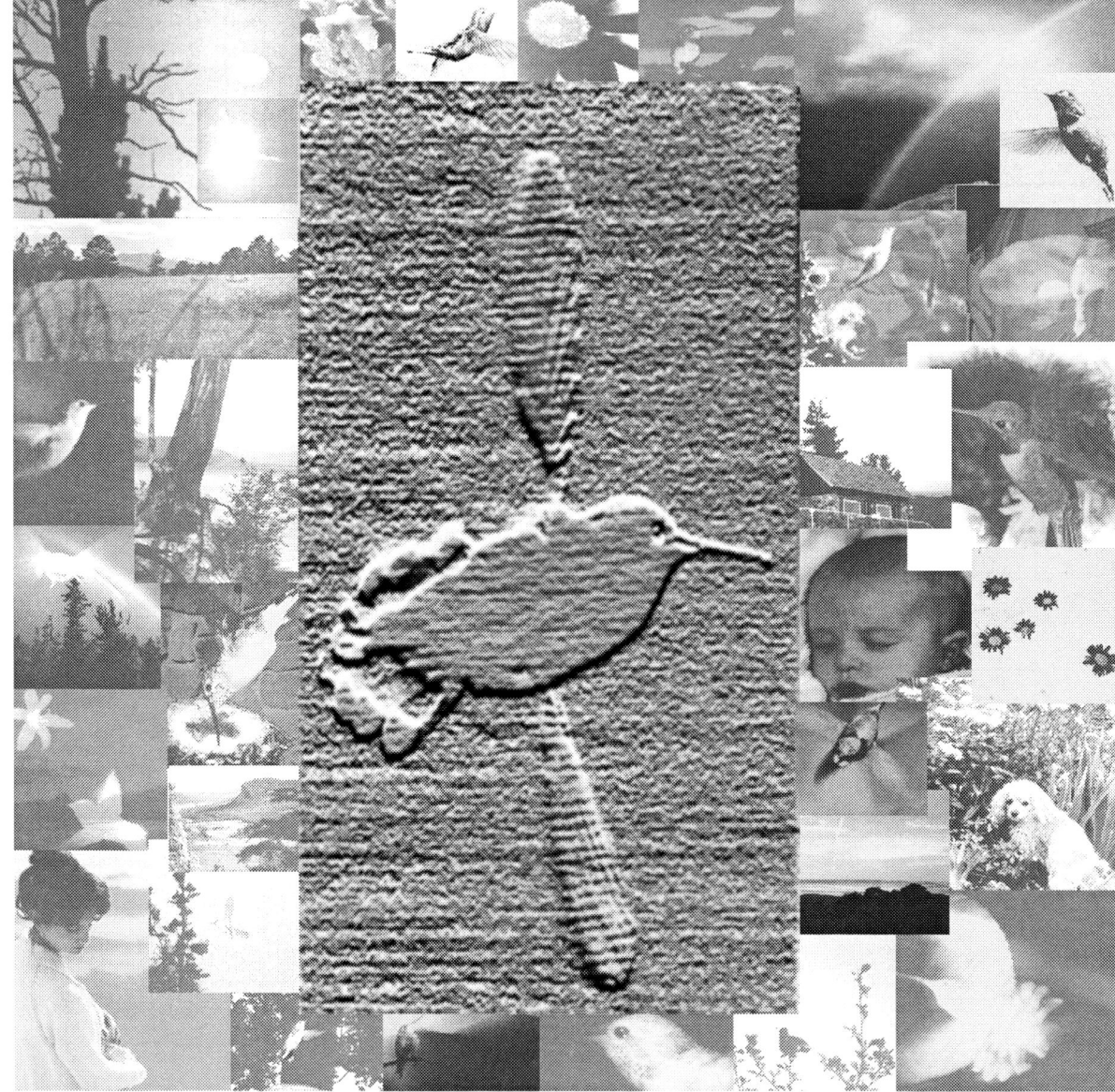

Iridescent Soul

The Story
The Music

M. L Stevens

How precious
Those jeweled little critters,
Spirit like,
Shimmering in the sun,
Decked with ruby, emerald,
Copper, and pearl,
Sailing across the sky
With the blaze of
Ten thousand golden sunrises!

For all who hold life very dearly,
and for my family,
especially my wife and two sons

Cascading off the slopes of the highest peaks, the breeze whispered messages of change. The firs rustled, the aspen quaked, and a mother hummingbird, perched in the tallest tree at the edge of the ledge, moved her head quickly back and forth, listening carefully.

Behind her, in the shadows 12 feet above the forest floor, her three-week-old nestlings preened their feathers and whirred their wings. Excitement gleamed in their eyes as they tottered and tested their ability to fly beside their stretched and nearly ruptured nest.

In a day or two, they would be in the alpine meadows discovering which flowers contained the sweetest nectar and what insects they could safely hawk. Before summer's end, they would have to begin the 2,000-mile migration to a warmer climate.

Each autumn for seven years, their mother had made the southward journey. And each spring, she had returned to these same mountains to raise two broods.

But now, she was beginning to feel her age. The growing weariness, the subtle quiverings, the stabs of pain—she could not deny.

One warm night, a week after her fledglings had left their nest the final time, she dreamed about the wintering grounds far to the south. Stirring restlessly, she opened her eyes to see a meteor blaze through the atmosphere. The image of the Master Hummingbird sweeping across the sky, beckoning her southward, flashed through her thought.

Looking out at the moonlit heavens, she began to feel an indescribable urge. Her heart thumped faster and her soul began to sing.

Promises

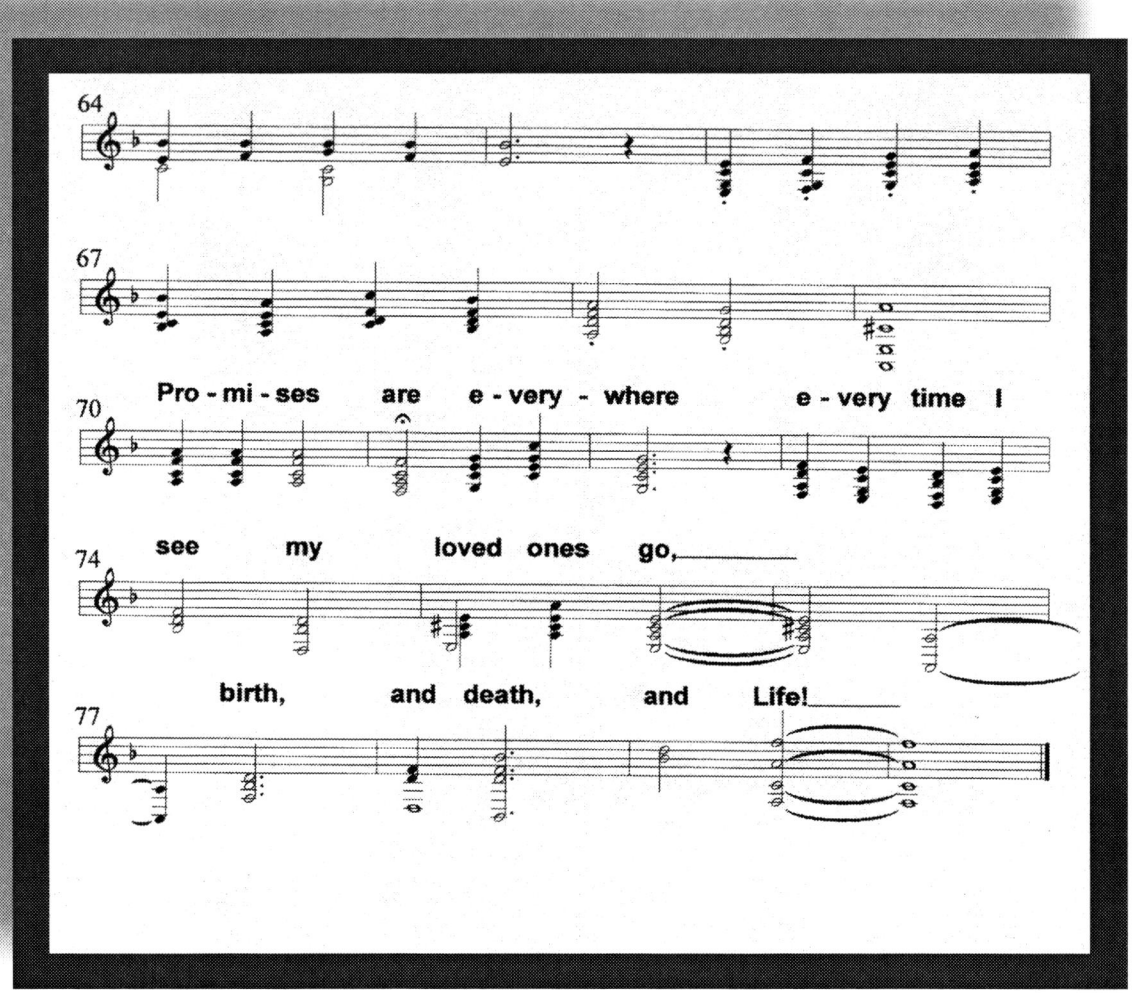

By early morning, the urge was pressing, the direction clear.

And so, as crows cawed, and eagles soared high, and marmots whistled across the slide rock, the hummingbird left her hillside home.

Leaving the burdens of motherhood behind, she set out through the rising mist. Soaring between two high granite cliffs like a leaf picked up by the wind, she dropped over the waterfall into the canyon below.

For two days she stopped only for food and water, and to catch her breath. Often she paused where the depth and breadth of the deepest woods were full of light.

The third morning, she perched on a branch of an ancient tree overlooking a familiar river valley. She ruffled her feathers to gather the feel of the overhead sun, of moisture in the air, of any hint of distant weather patterns. She listened to the direction of passing insects, to birds' whistles and squawks, to the wind passing through the trees.

The air movement shifted and so did her thoughts. She was on her own now, an explorer on her final journey. But why was she so anxious to get to the winter feeding grounds ahead of the others? Summer was not suddenly going to disapear.

Excitement brewing, she flexed her wings and shot out across the river toward new territory—toward a greatness she could only feel.

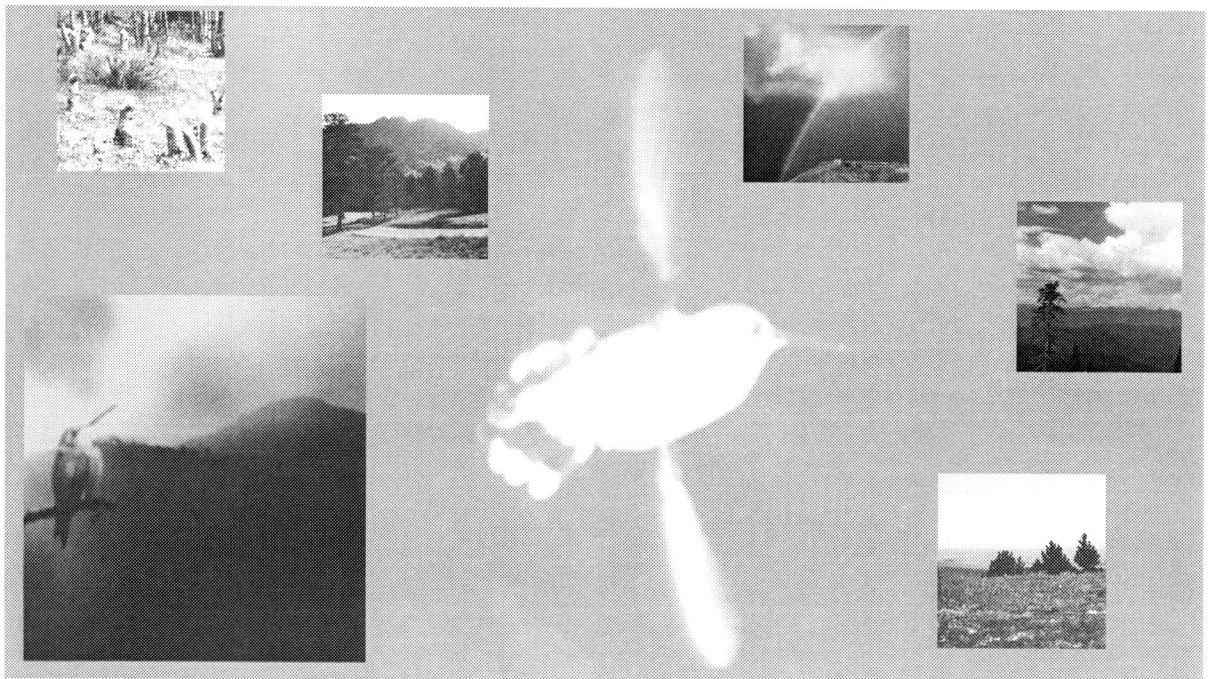

Wandering

(Adapted from a 20th century traditional Christmas song by John Jacob Niles)

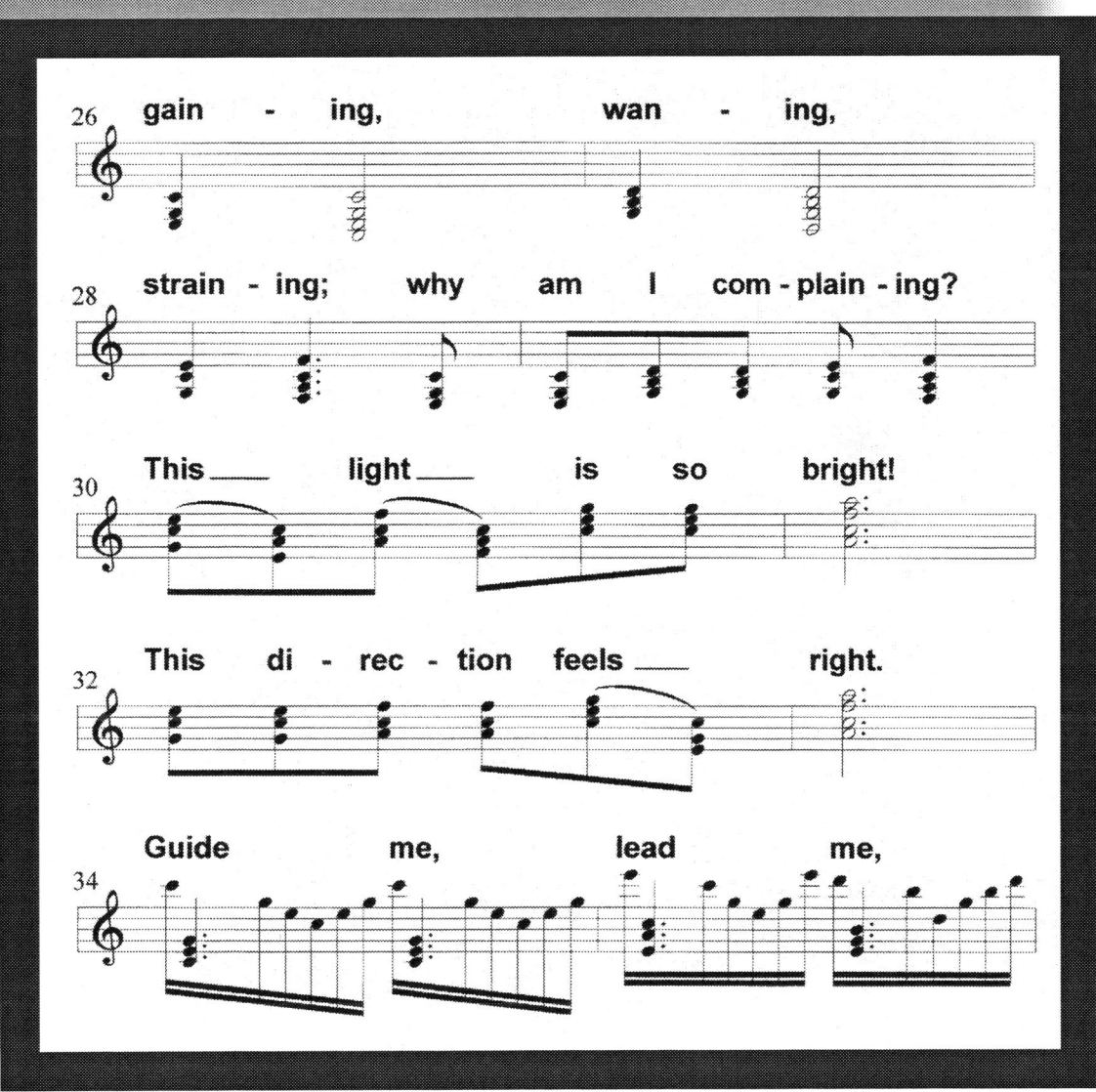

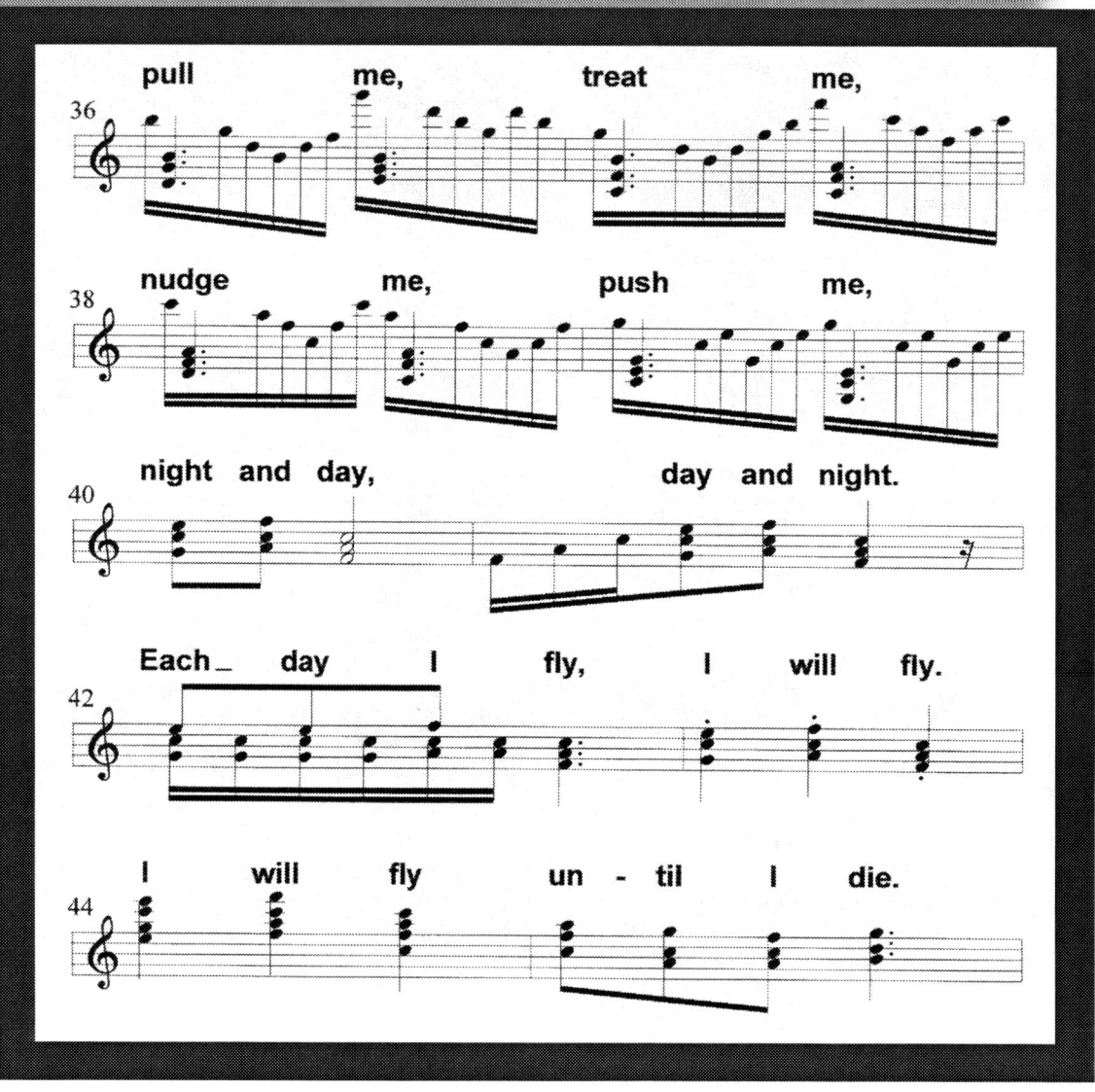

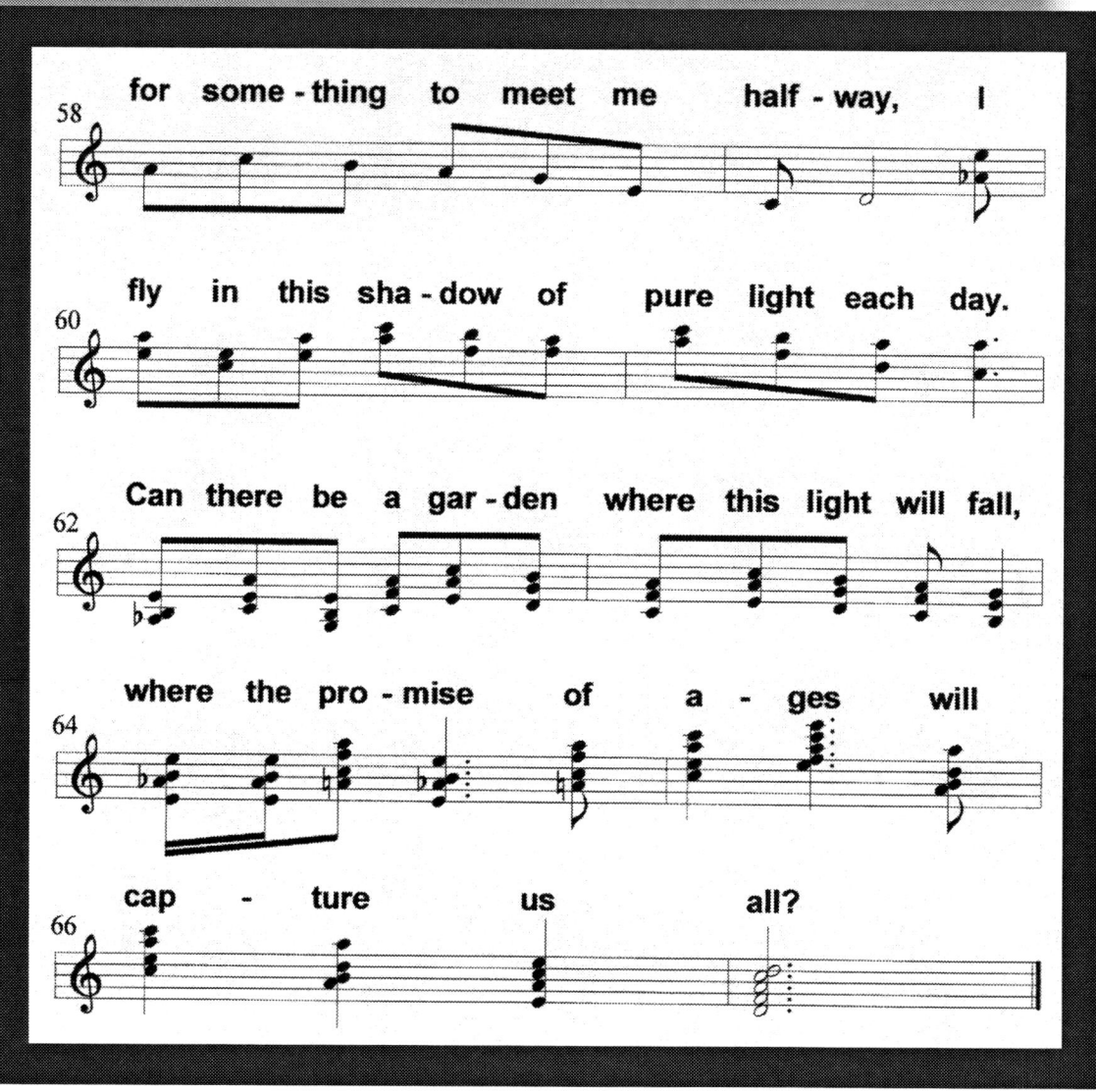

That afternoon past high plateaus, she came upon abandoned fields infested with purple thistles. She feasted on the nectar, careful not to get caught in the thick, wiry heads.

Pushing on, she flew past junipers and sagebrush, across herds of cattle chewing their cuds, over scrub oak and pine trees.

Cresting a ridge, she approached a fieldstone house. Hovering above it, she stared down at the bright red-shingled roof. For a hummingbird, red was a most promising color.

Weary from her flight, wearier than she had ever been, she let her wings fold. When her feet touched the rooftop, she closed her eyes and cheeped a sigh of relief.

Evening came. A slight breeze rustled her feathers and she steadied her feet under her. Barely able to lift off the roof, she drifted toward the pine tree shading the corner of the house.

In the thick branches of needles, she peered down—and blinked with disbelief. There, stretching the length of the house, was a forest of flowers! A fence was covered with honeysuckle, and a trumpet vine draped a dead tree trunk. Butterfly bushes and daisies and other flowers stretched away from the house. Tall spikes of maroon, red, pink, and white hollyhocks were everywhere.

Trembling from her good fortune, she dove into the thicket and thrust her beak into the heart of a maroon hollyhock. The nectar was deliciously sweet. Flowing smoothly down her throat, it created a warm glow. Whipping her tongue across her beak, she moved to a red hollyhock, an orange trumpet vine, and then to several pink and white honeysuckle.

Feeling a newness surge through her veins, she perched on a clothesline stretching alongside the flowers, parallel to the house. Scanning back and forth, she joyfully inspected the garden. Could there be enough flowers here to feed her the rest of the summer? She wiped the pollen off her beak with her claw, then stopped to listen.

In some tree nearby, a woodpecker hammered with its powerful beak. Swallows swept by, chirping as they filled their craws with insects. A young sparrow poked its head out of the hollow clothesline crossbar nearest her.

So much for the other birds. Only one thing concerned her now. As far as she could tell, the garden was all her own. No other hummingbird had staked out these flowers.

Garden

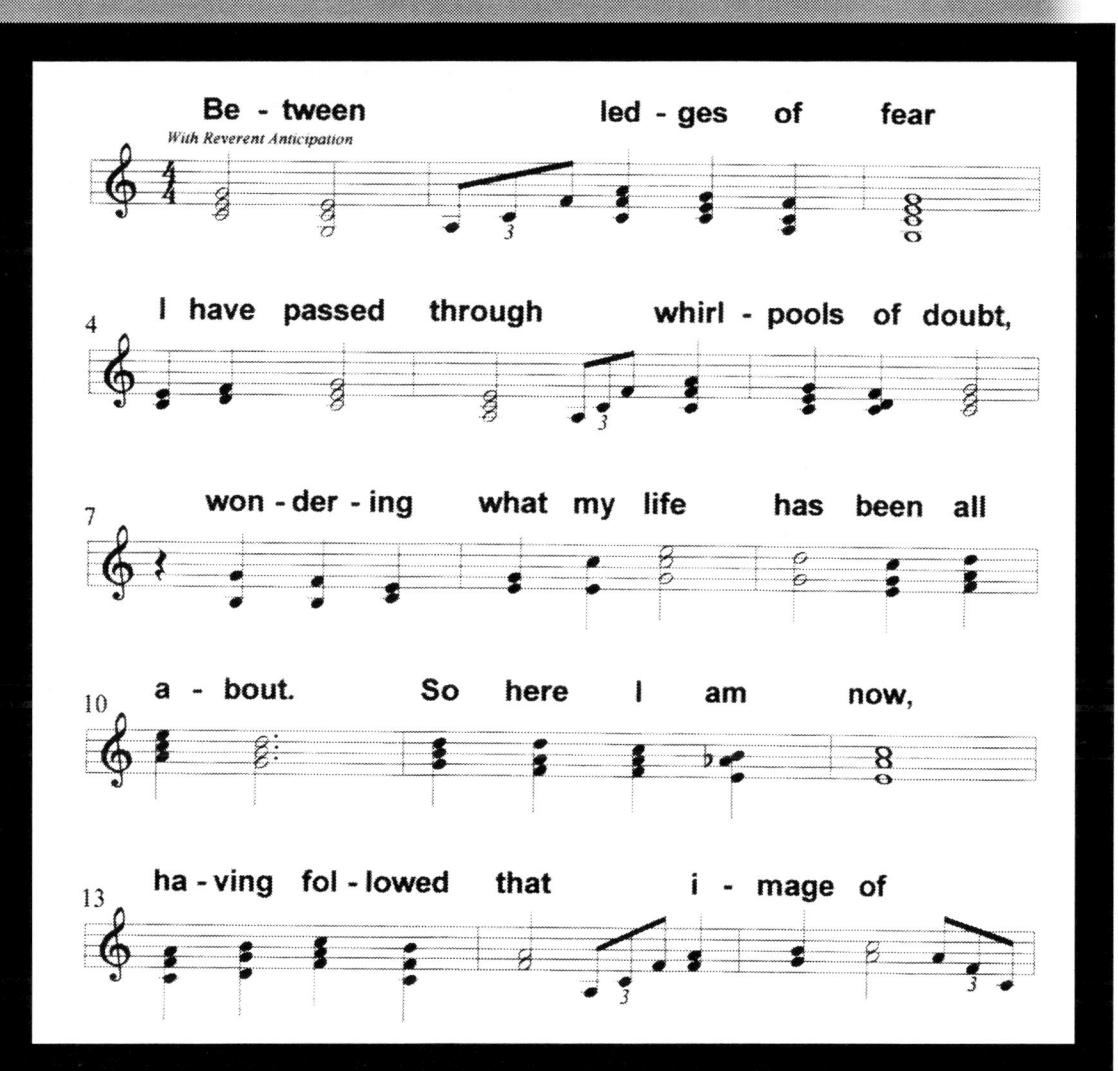

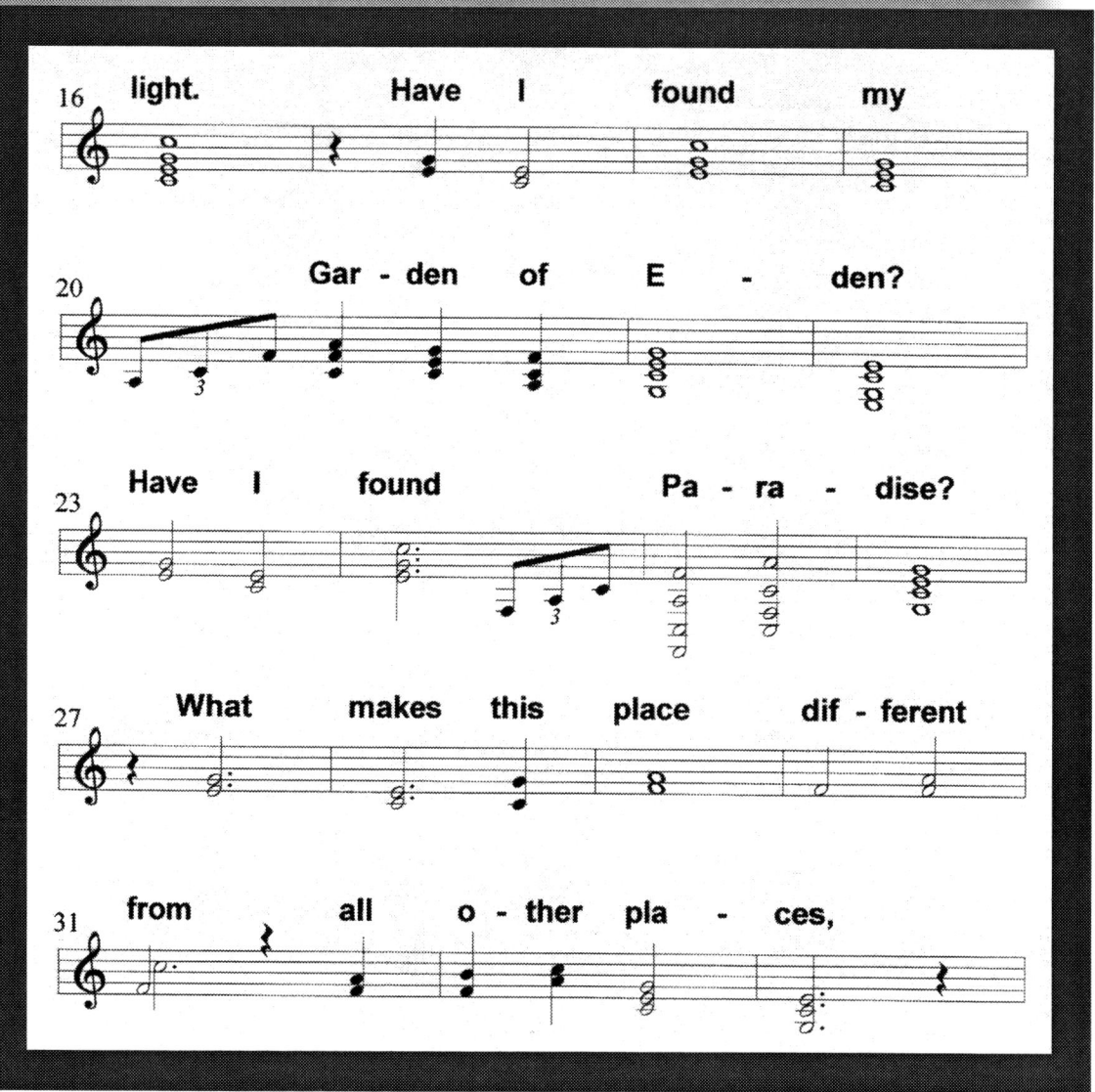

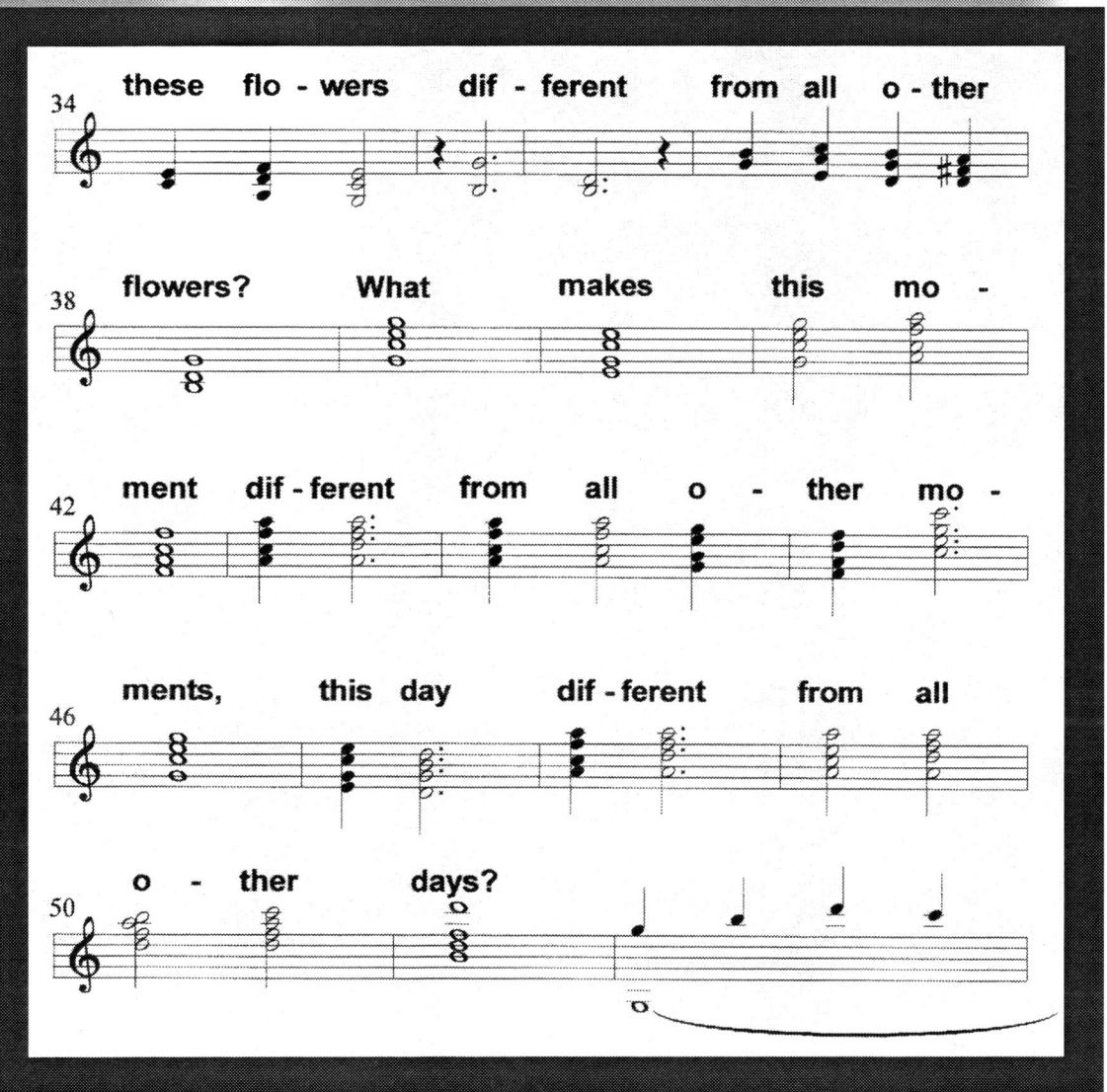

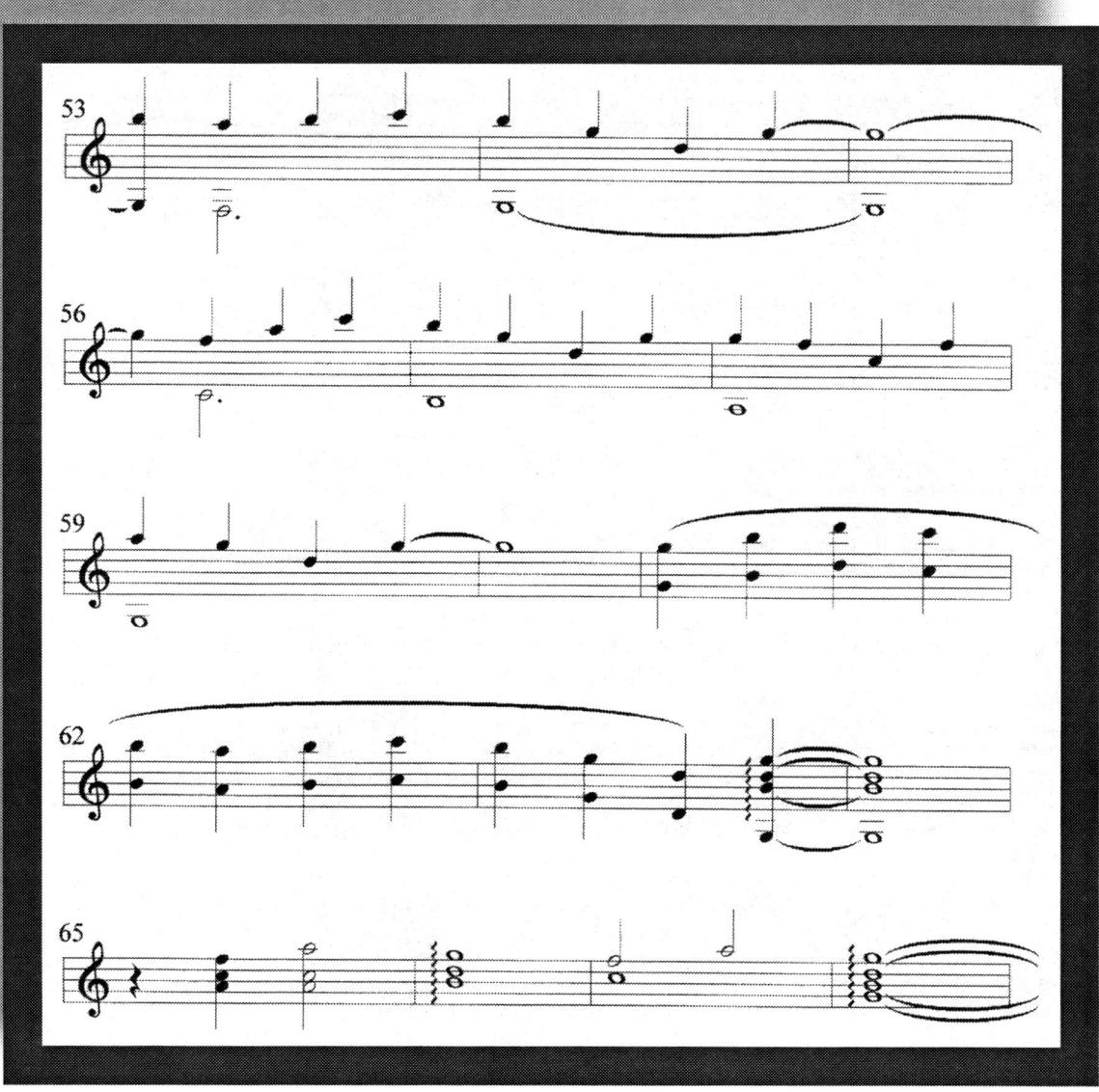

As beams of morning light filtered through the tree and radiated off the roof, she stirred slowly from her torpid sleep—aware in degrees of warmth and the solidity of her body.

Responding to the whisper of the flowers' welcoming song, she dropped out of the tree and brushed thankfully against the petals with her breast. Filling herself with sweet nectar, she felt rejuvenated.

Circling the house, she hovered near the windows, certain she saw glimpses of her youthful self. Perching on the rooftop, she marveled at the crispness of the morning air. Her senses were sharp, her imagination lit.

She pondered the dream of the night before. In it, every one of her nestlings had grown into a healthy fledgling, leaving the nest on its own. No accident, storm, or hungry predator had forced her to start over. What a family of hummingbirds she had seen on the hillside!

Yet, there had been the one empty nest.

She returned to the clothesline and stared across the flowers. On the ground beneath her, dozens of young sparrows bounced along, pecking rambunctiously through the sticks and grit for food. Suddenly, they shot upward like a wave of chattering dirt clods and rose as one away from the house.

Moments later, two upright creatures appeared and the hummingbird darted to her tree. Dashing under the clothesline, the boy and a younger girl ran their hands along the two lines, then headed toward the barn.

A pregnant woman, carrying a brown basket, stepped off the porch followed by an old dog. Both walked along the house under the tree, directly beneath the hummingbird.

Setting the basket down at the end of the clothesline, the woman pulled a hollyhock to her nose and sighed loudly. Reaching into the brown basket, she began to sort, shake out, and hang up her family's wet laundry.

The hummingbird watched curiously.

Detached feathers, perhaps? But the woman's flapping the wet clothes did not lift her into the air.

A mating ritual, perhaps? But then, as with hummingbirds, was it not the male that displayed the nuptial colors?

Nesting material, perhaps? But the woman was taking from the basket, not adding to it.

When the garden was quiet, the hummingbird hovered between the sagging lines, inspecting the limp clothes, intrigued by the dampness of the air. She settled between two clothespins where she could see the flowers and began to preen her own feathers.

Late that afternoon, the hummingbird watched the woman remove the dry clothes and place them in the basket. The upright creature's movements were precise and calculated—as if shadowing an expectant hummingbird gathering material for a nest.

Again, the hummingbird remembered her dream.

As the disappearing sun cast a yellow glow across the evening sky, she remained hidden in her tree. Ruffling her feathers and scanning her surroundings, she became bewildered at the growing feeling of responsibility pounding in her chest.

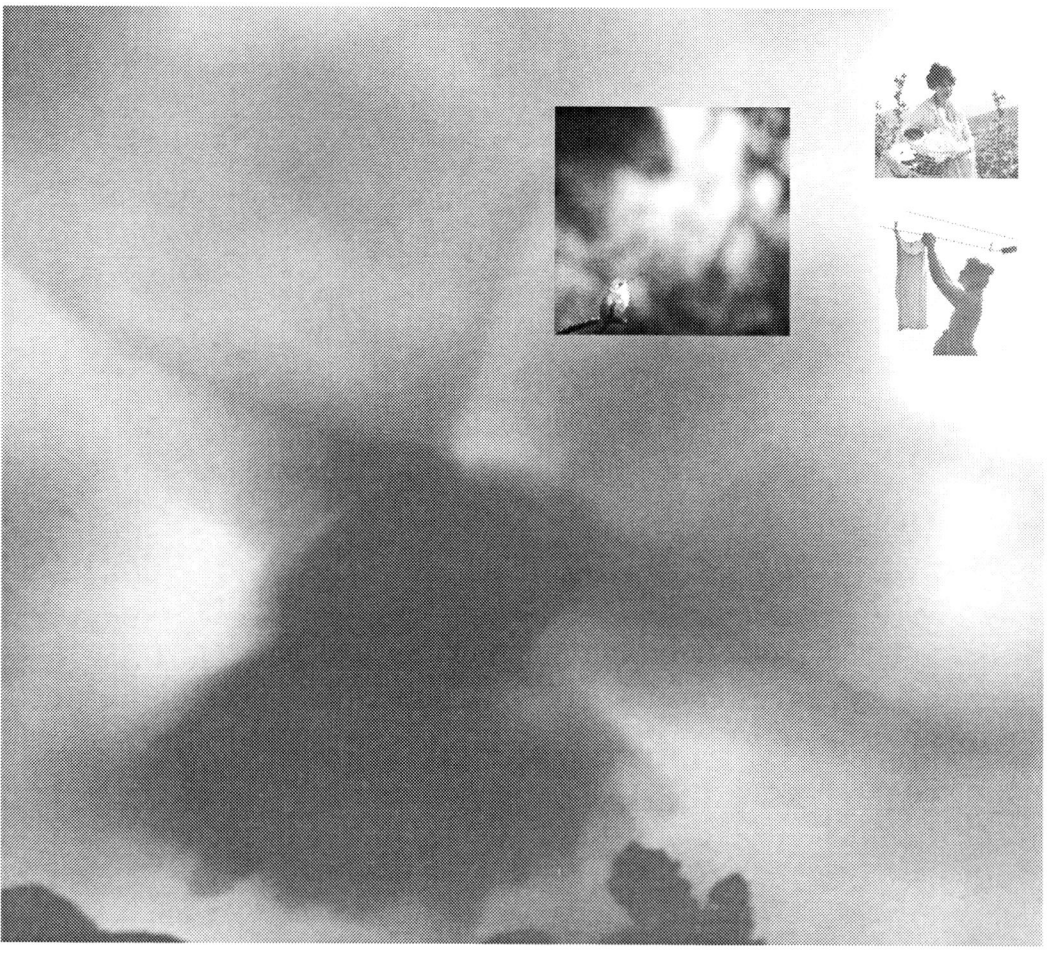

Going Back

(Part 1)

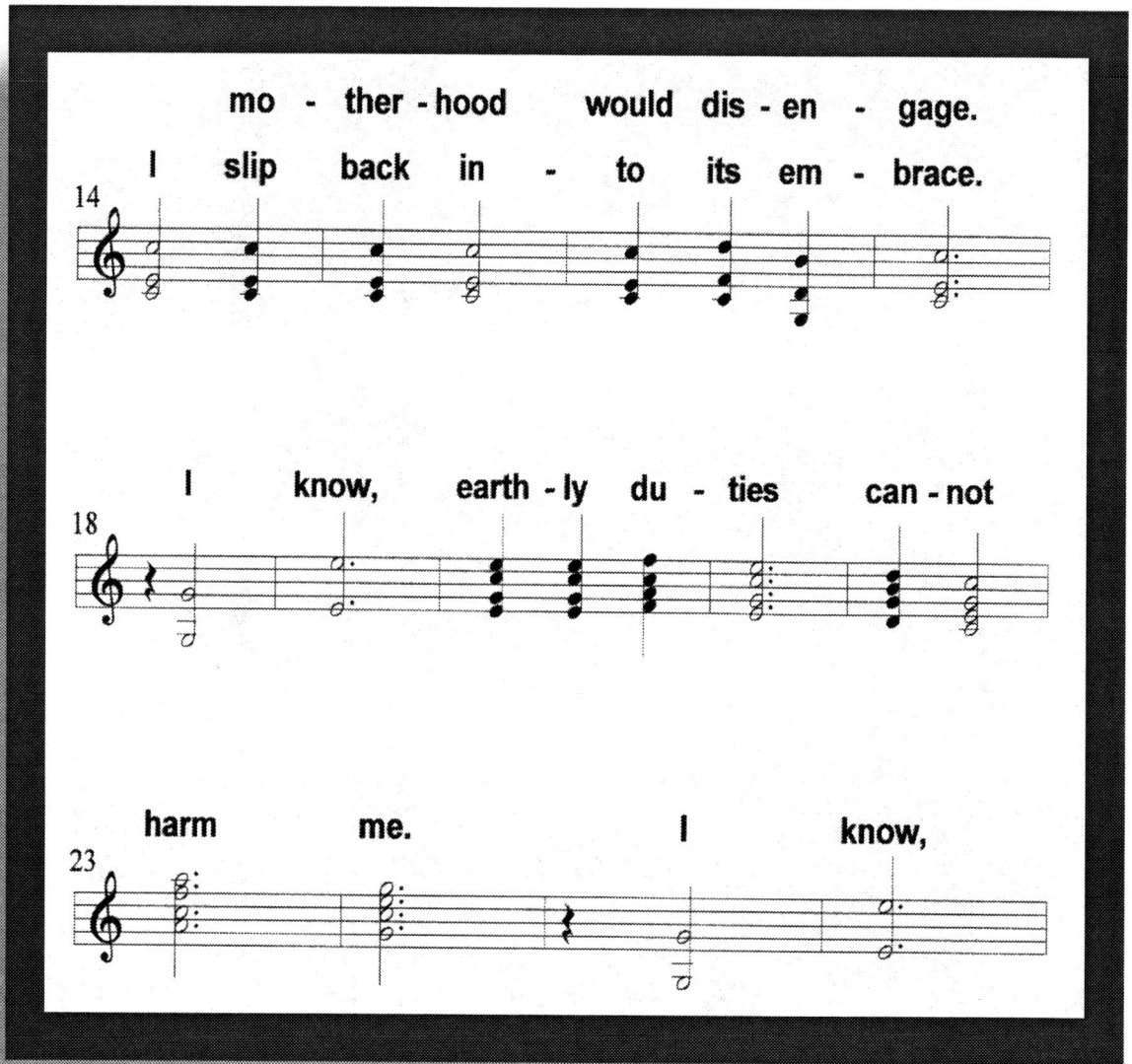

26

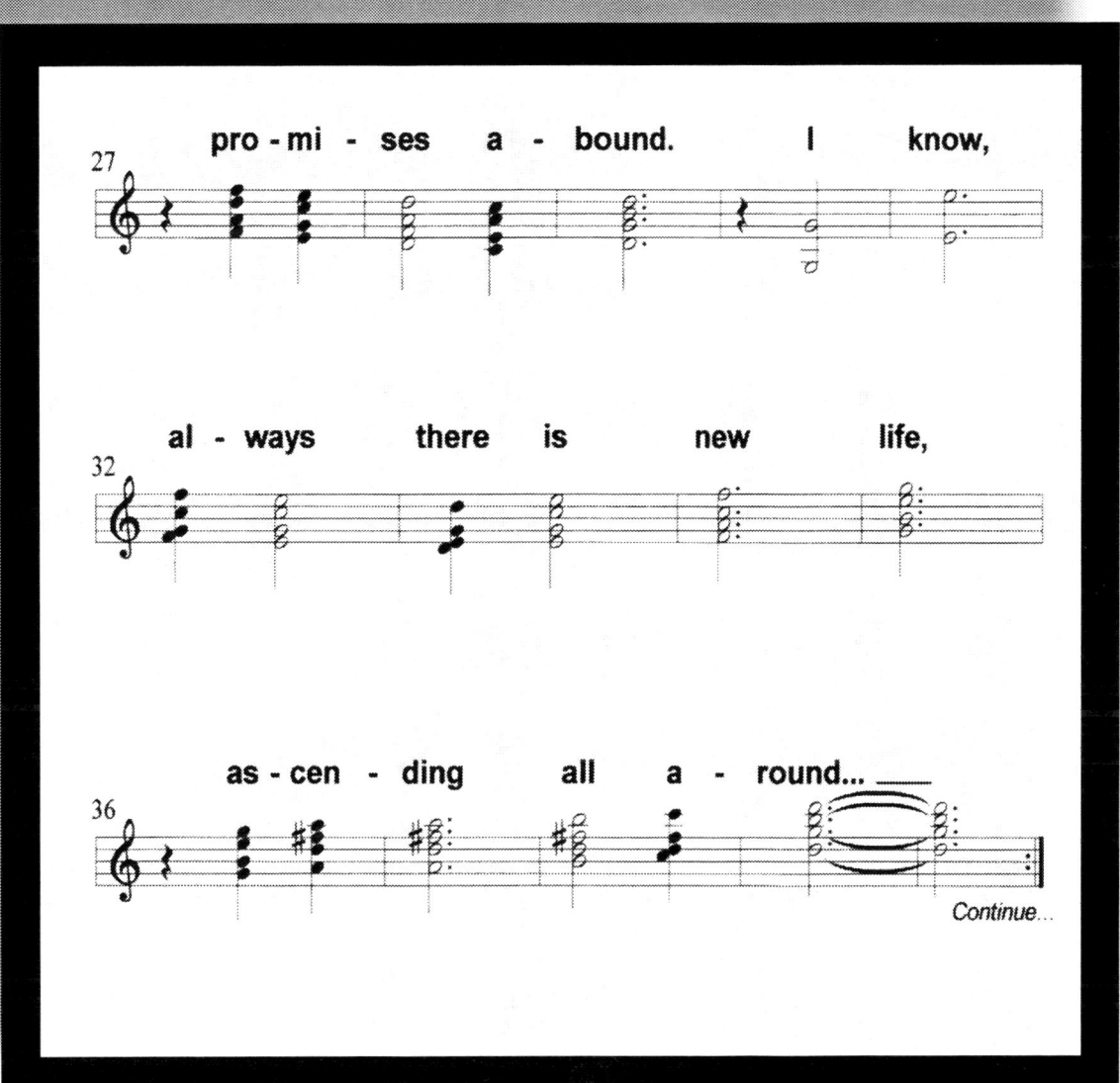

She surveyed her garden from many angles—from the flowers, the clothesline, the edge of the roof, and from her tree. She checked different branches for approach, sturdiness, view, and concealment. One spot she measured over and over with her wings, picturing herself there sitting on a throne.

Materials were plentiful. For the bulk of her nest, she captured seed fluff from nearby dandelions, milkweed, and thistle. She also used hunks of bark from her tree, and animal hair from a nearby fence. Under the eave of the house, she found plenty of spider webs to tie her throne together and secure it to the branch.

Fussy and determined, she sat in the middle and built a mound around herself— pressing, fluffing, poking. As she worked, she envisioned herself as the oldest hummingbird on earth, surrounded with phantoms of unborn hummingbirds cheeping loudly to come into the world.

The next day was wretchedly hot and, sipping wearily from the hollyhocks, she had second thoughts about finishing her nest.

Hovering near the house, she stared at a window, watching the reflection of herself. Might she be deceiving herself? She backed away, staring at the house from a distance. What could be in this final round of motherhood for her?

Back on the clothesline, she stared across the flowers and thought back as far as she could to her many broadtail mates. Pensive images flowed from her heart and filled her head.

Going Back

(Part 2)

32

Late the next day, she watched her garden as usual from the clothesline when the high trill from the slot-tipped wings of a male reached across the valley. Clutching the wire tightly, she twitched her tail, fluttered her wings, and flicked her head.

Suddenly there was a shadow—and silence. Spinning furiously around, she almost missed the wire, grabbing it with one foot as a rush of excitement overwhelmed her.

On the other line, a male broadtail stared intensely at her with dark eyes. With burning impatience and a growing desire, he barreled his chest, ruffled his feathers and fluttered his wings—his iridescence shimmering with fire.

Her vulnerability was obvious, inviting attention. Both knew it was moments like this when a strong female could resist matter-of-factly, or when a male could lay claim to the nuptial rights.

Nuptials

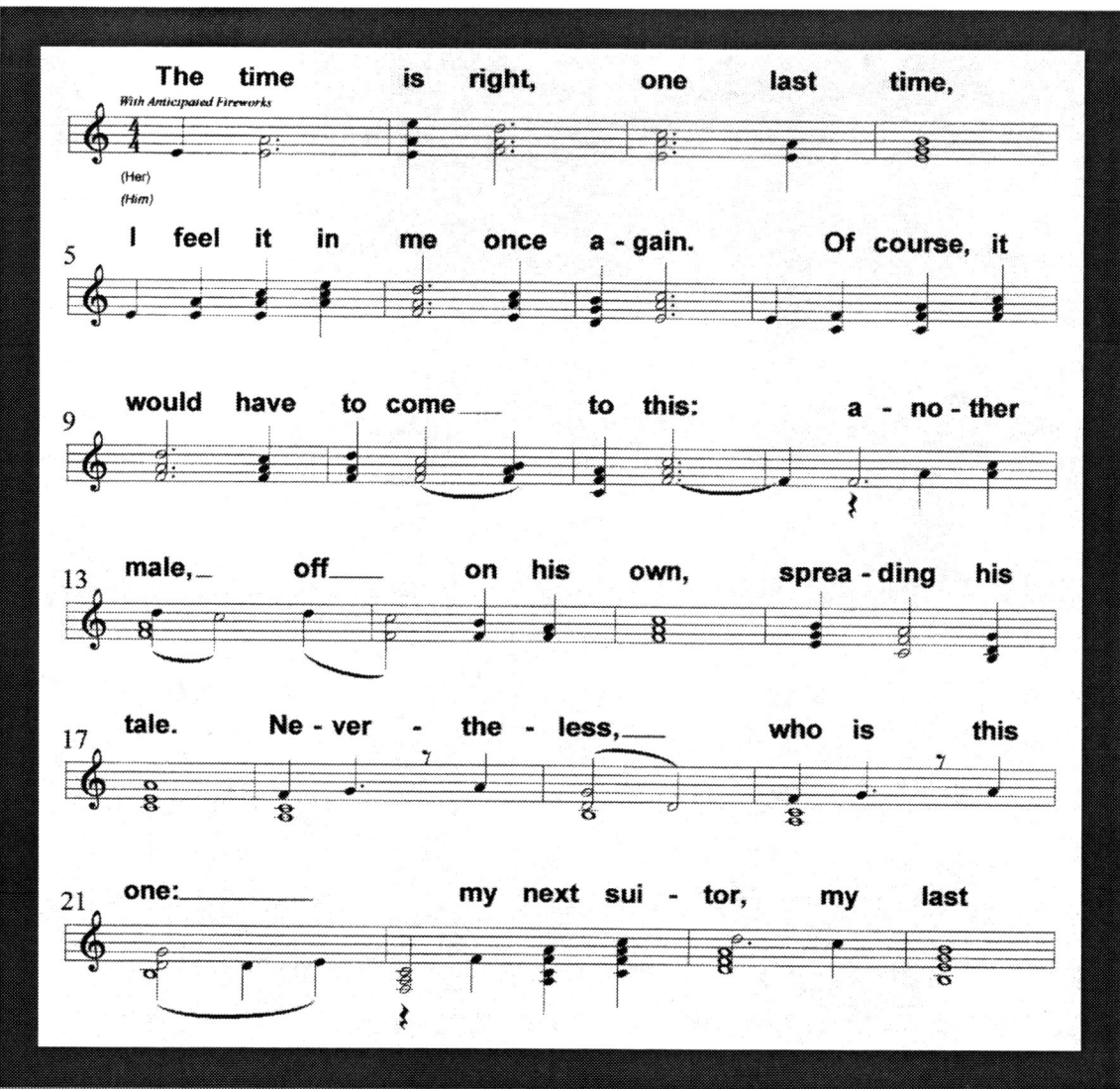

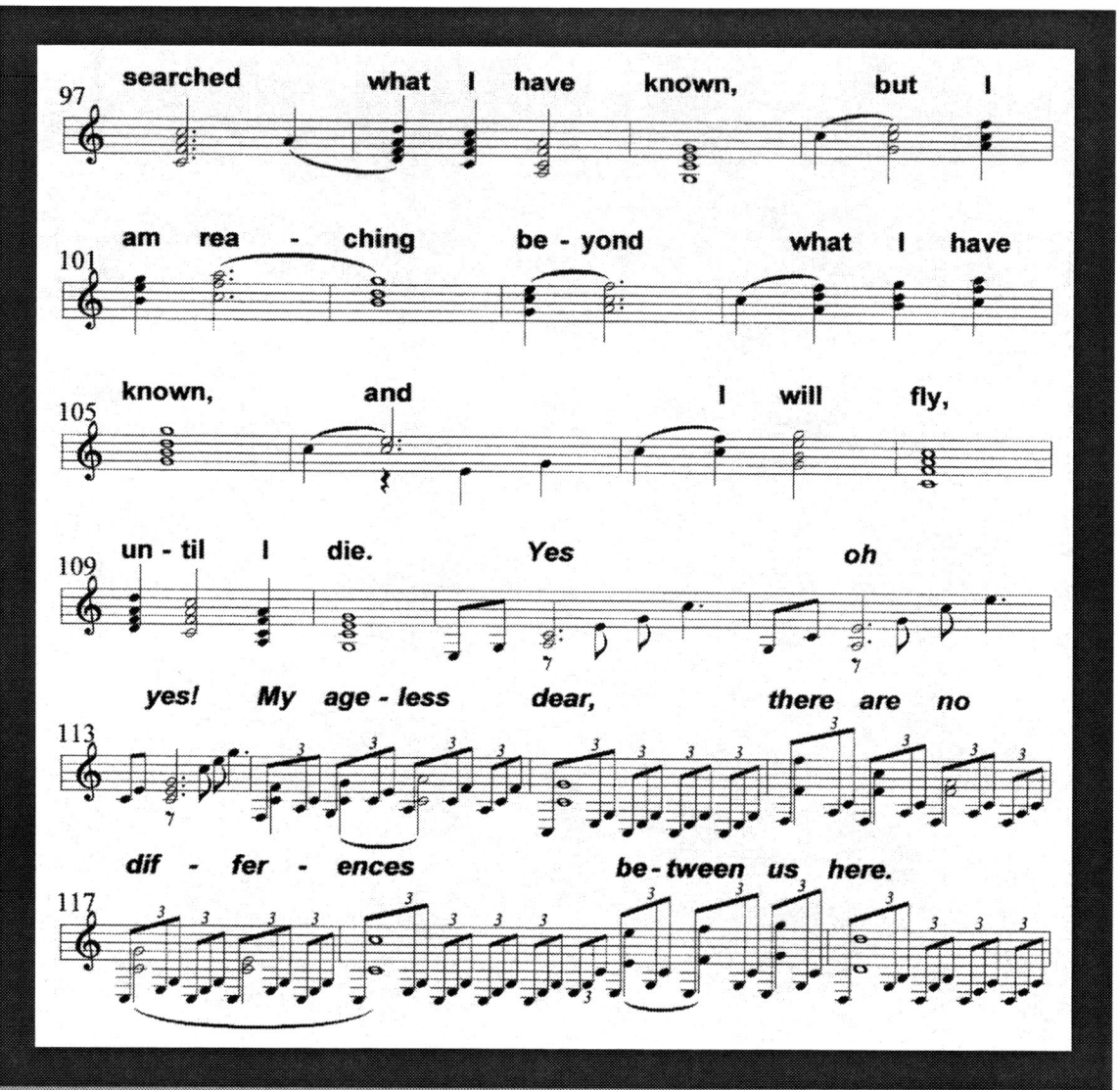

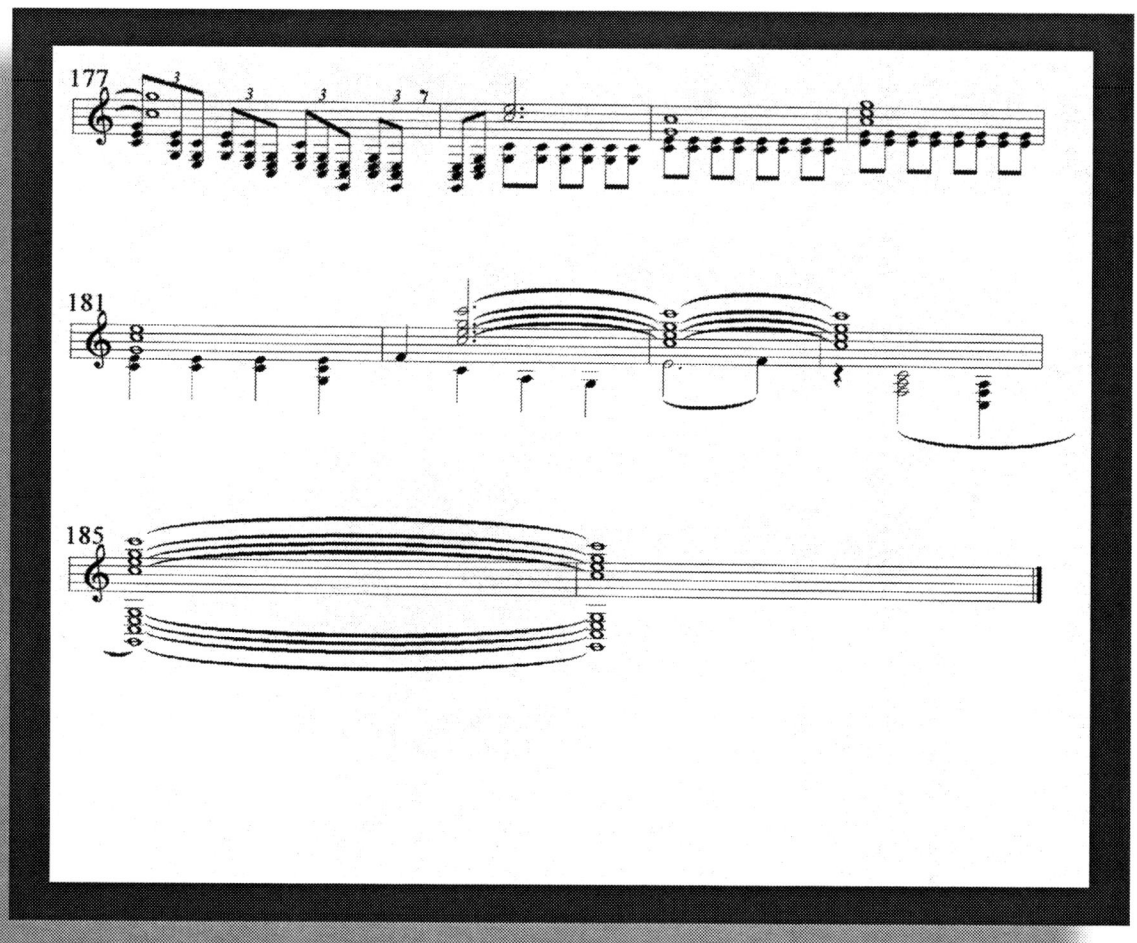

And so, as the sun splashed gold across the evening sky, he shuttled past her, drumming his tail loudly in her face, and shot upward into a large oval loop. Rushing past her, he cheeped and rattled his wings and tail. Again and again he made the oval dive. Each time he passed her, he spread his maroon gorget so it would catch the full brightness of sunset's glow.

After his fifth dive, she rose off the clothesline and reached him 50 feet above the house. Facing each other, they danced, rose away from each other, and met again, dancing more intensely.

Yes, how could she not be impressed?

That night after he was gone and she had preened her feathers, she settled into her unfinished nest. As she stared upward, the images of his presence would not go away.

Just One

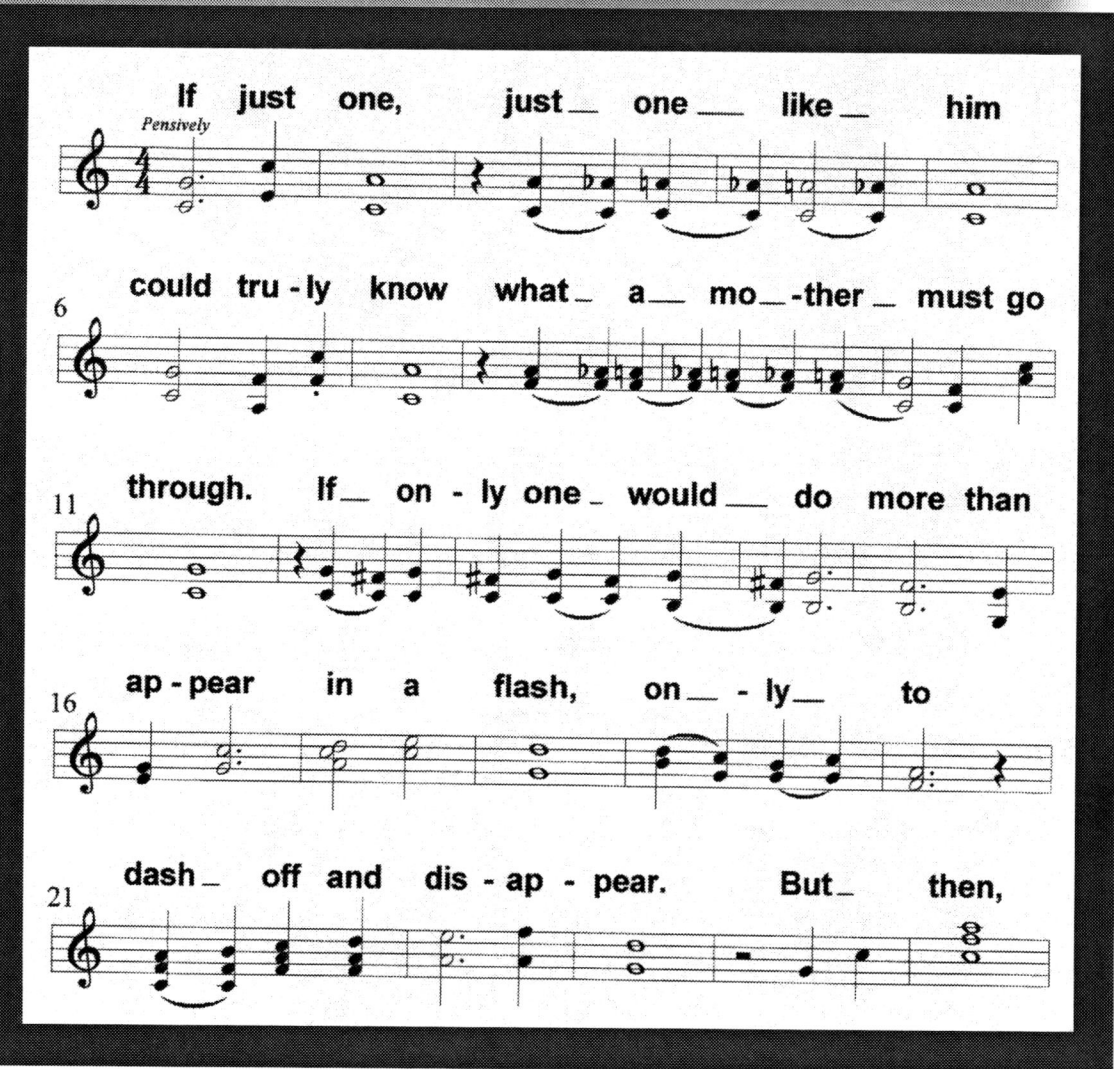

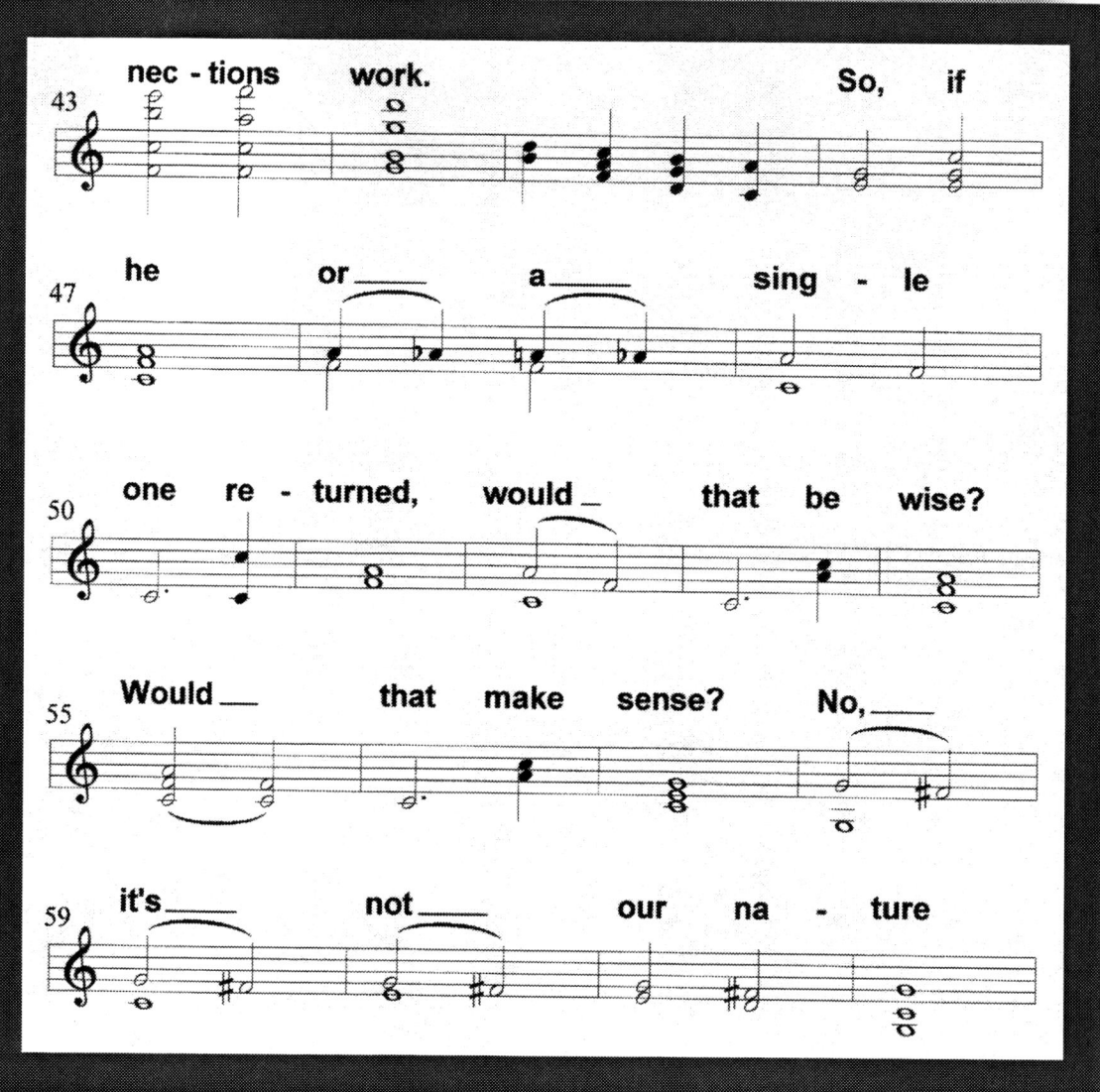

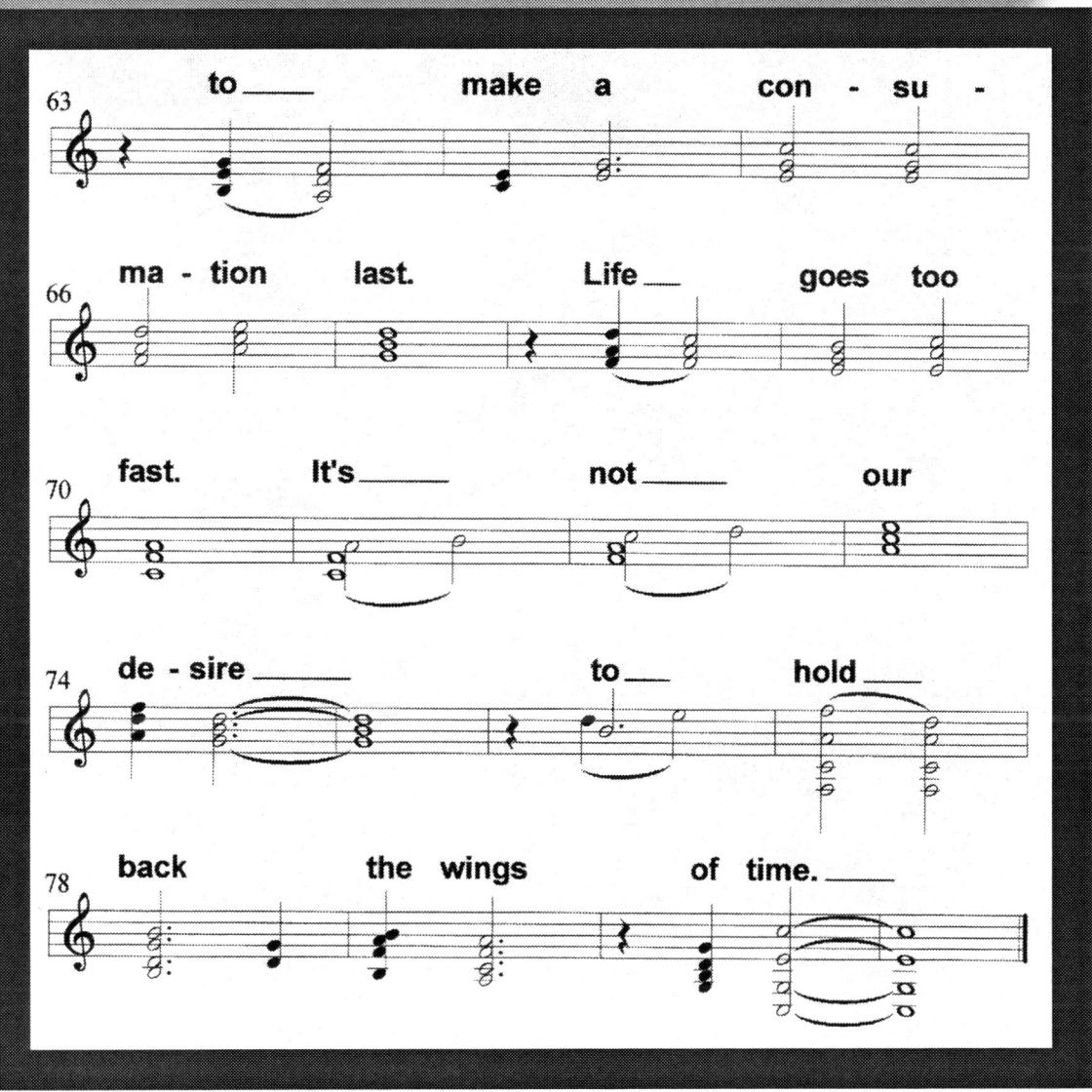

As dawn's pink glow edged the horizon, the hummingbird fluttered to the top of the roof and looked eastward. Breathing deeply, she felt a quiet sense of relief. No doubt about it: a spark of life was once again forming inside her.

Her final building task was to camouflage the outside of her throne. All day she attempted, with pieces of leaf and bark, to match the color and pattern of the fieldstone in the wall of the house. The result looked pretty much like her other nests.

Early the next morning she fluttered restlessly among the flowers, and back and forth between the clothesline and the top of the roof. Unable to escape the quickening contractions, she flew to her throne and clung to its edge. Her breath came shallowly, then in rapid spurts. Fanned-out tail feathers quivering, vision blurring, she pointed her beak upward and aimed with all her strength toward the center of the nest.

48

Mother Earth

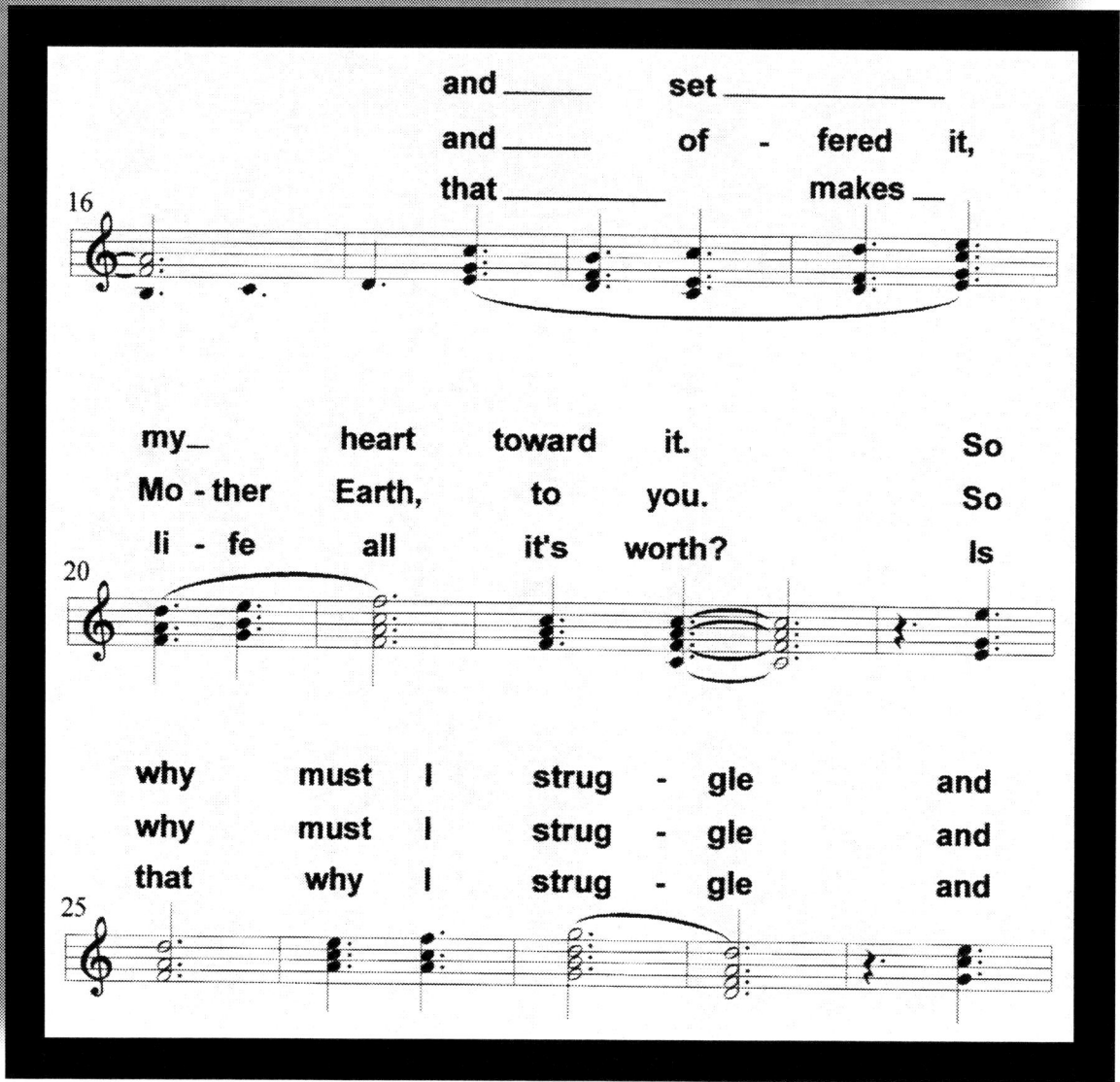

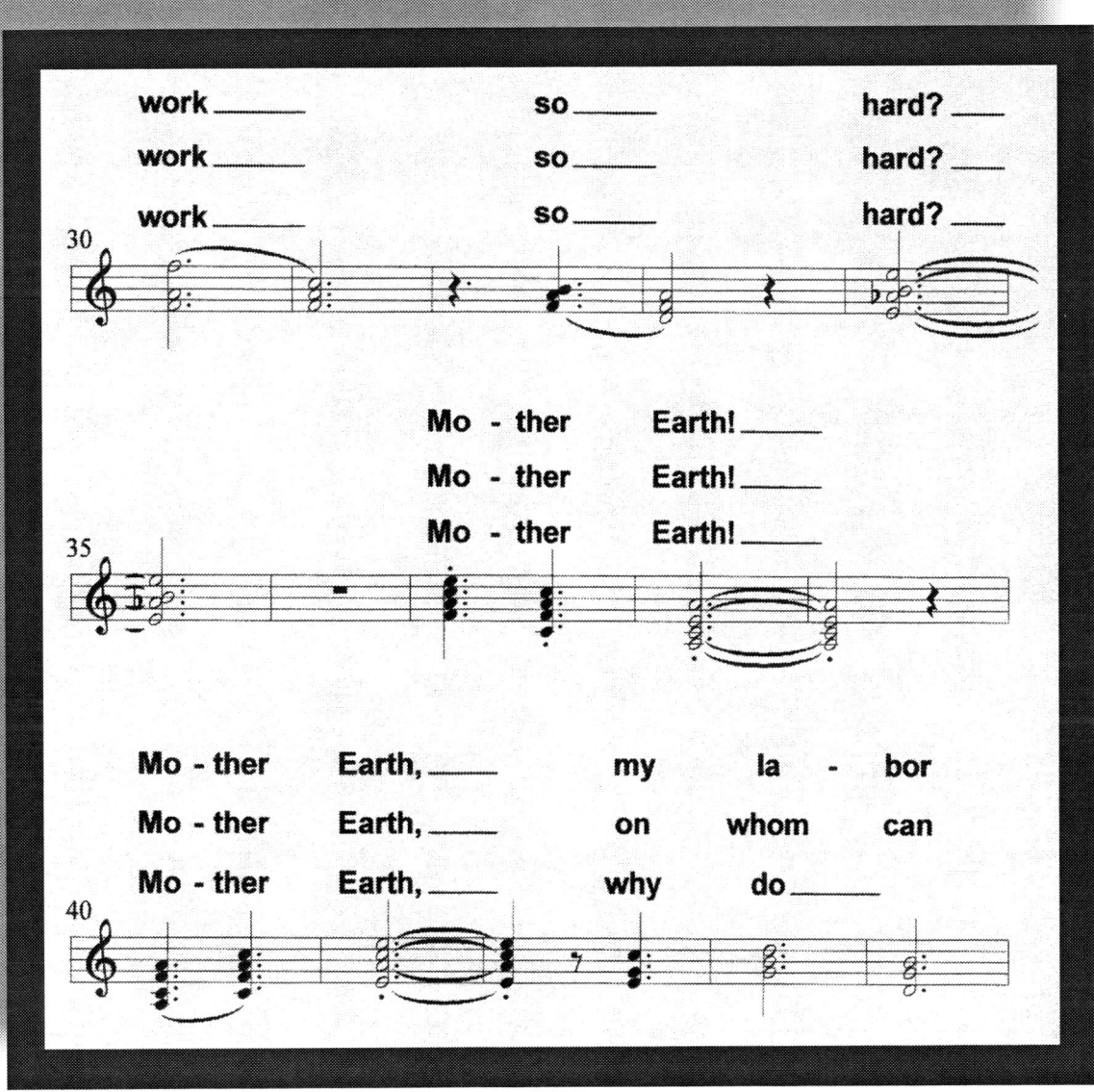

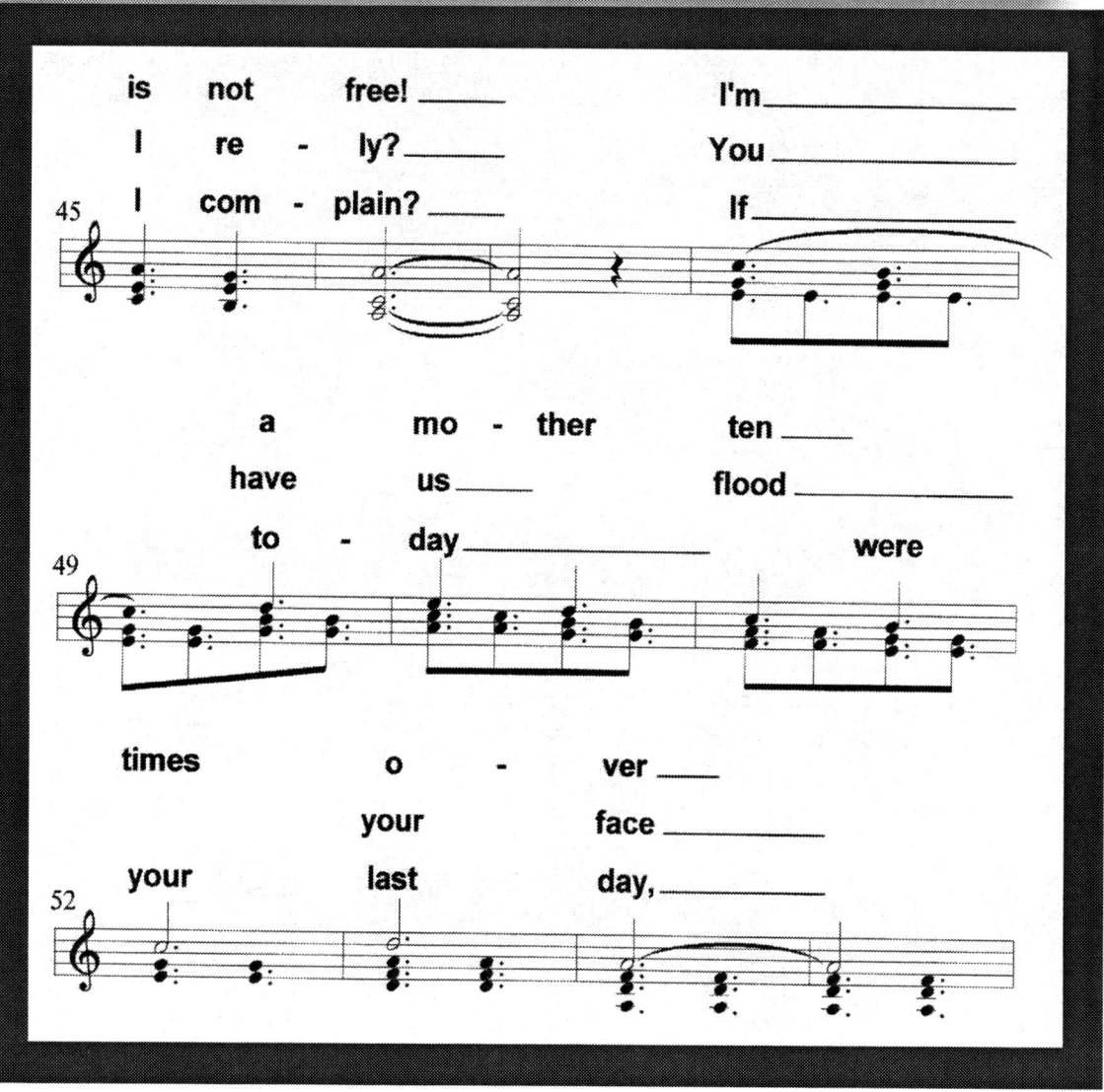

When the ordeal was over, she sank into her throne—trembling, a ragged heap.

Twenty minutes passed before she was able to rise up and inspect her egg. Pushing it back and forth with her beak, she tested its size and shape—a bit confused as to why this egg was larger than any she had ever produced.

She had never been patient at waiting, but 24 hours was needed before a second egg could pass.

And so, restlessly, she zigzagged all that day across the fields and through the hills. From flower to flower, from tree to tree, from hilltop to hilltop, images of birth and death appeared and reappeared.

The next morning, beside her nest, she woke with a start and looked around. There was no pressure, no circle of pain. Her body felt light and wispy like a detached leaf.

Always before, each time, she had brought two eggs into existence—a task she had always expected.

But this time, she realized, there was not going to be a second egg.

Fine. For once, Mother Earth was not making great demands. For once, Mother Earth was being kind.

One egg, less work, one less craw to fill. Incubation must begin immediately.

Life's Forming

(Celebrating the Native American Spirit)

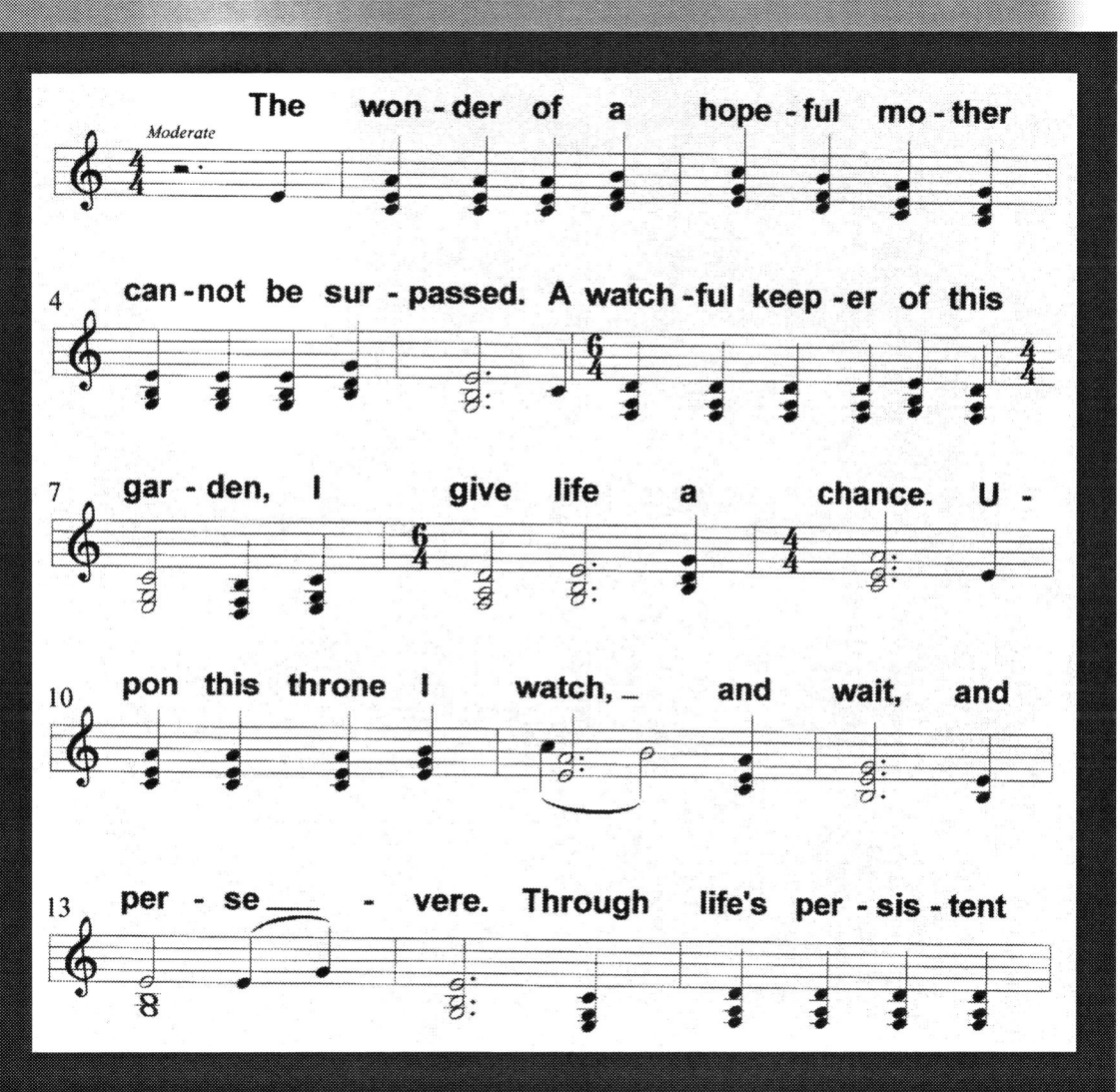

Each day, she left her nest at least 40 times to eat and drink. Many of the flowers continued to put out new blooms, and insects were drawn to them, and she fed continually.

Whenever the woman appeared with the brown laundry basket, or the boy and girl loitered in the flowers or near the tree, she remained motionless on her nest, remembering her young ones of summers past.

Five days into incubation, she began to feel the growing warmth under her. Every day she turned the egg over to keep her body heat spread evenly over it.

Life could be so warm, so bounteous. Now, in her garden, there was another resident. Besides the old dog, there was also a small pup. Obviously, it too was part of the family of upright creatures.

Halfway through the second week, she began to notice a palpable movement against her brood patch. More than once, she fluttered joyfully on the edge of her nest—a proud great-she-knew-not-how-many-times-great grandmother able to be a mother once again.

But something had always puzzled her: mainly, the egg's large size. As the time for hatching drew near, she sometimes found herself jolted from her reverie. Darting off her nest, she hovered—staring down, wondering. What was it that aroused her fear?

Sometimes it seemed as if two spirits were struggling under her, trapped inside the same shell.

But, no, that could not happen. Never had it happened to her.

With trepidation, she left the nest less often, hurrying to the flowers only when her needs were urgent.

Apprehension

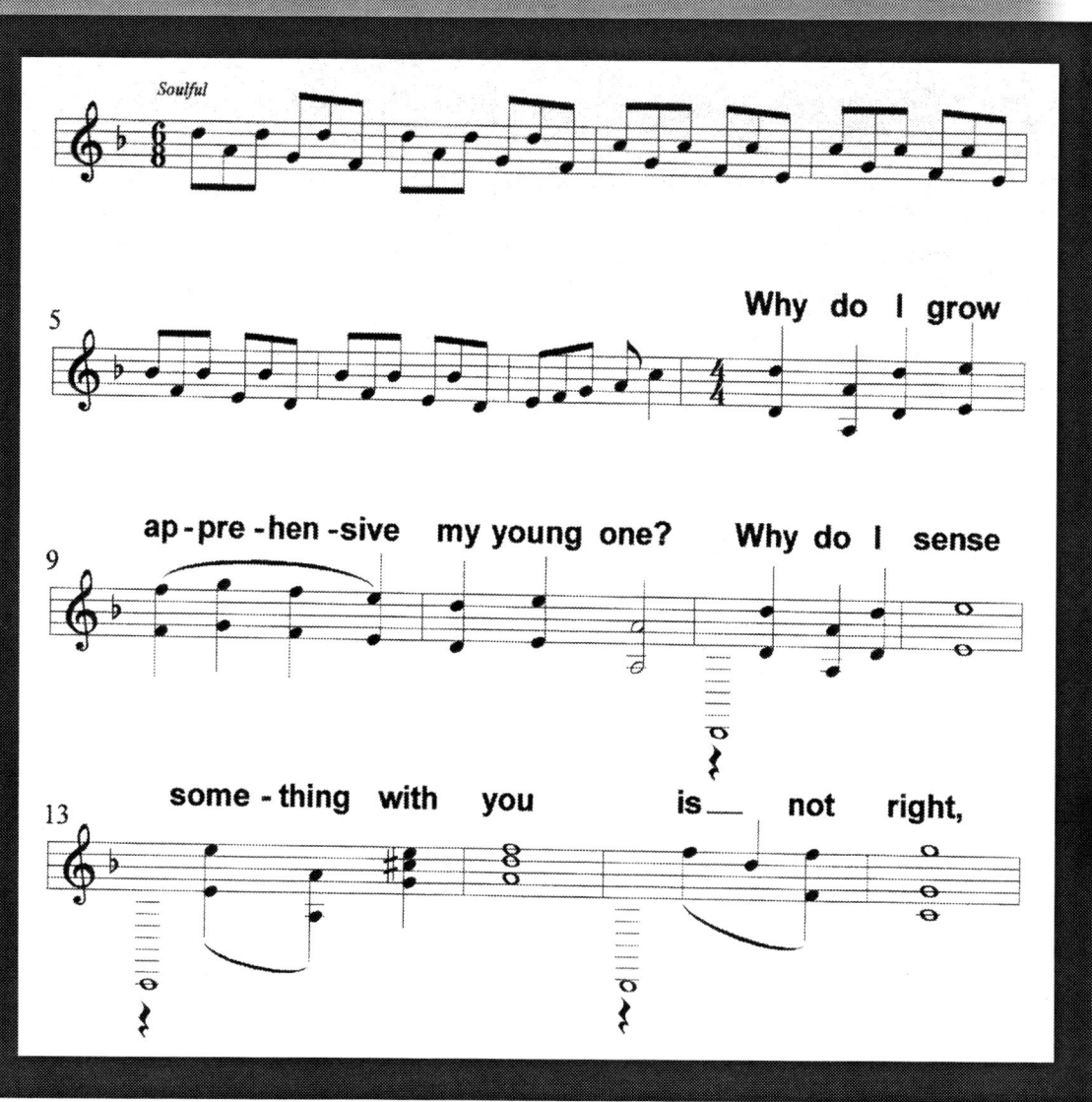

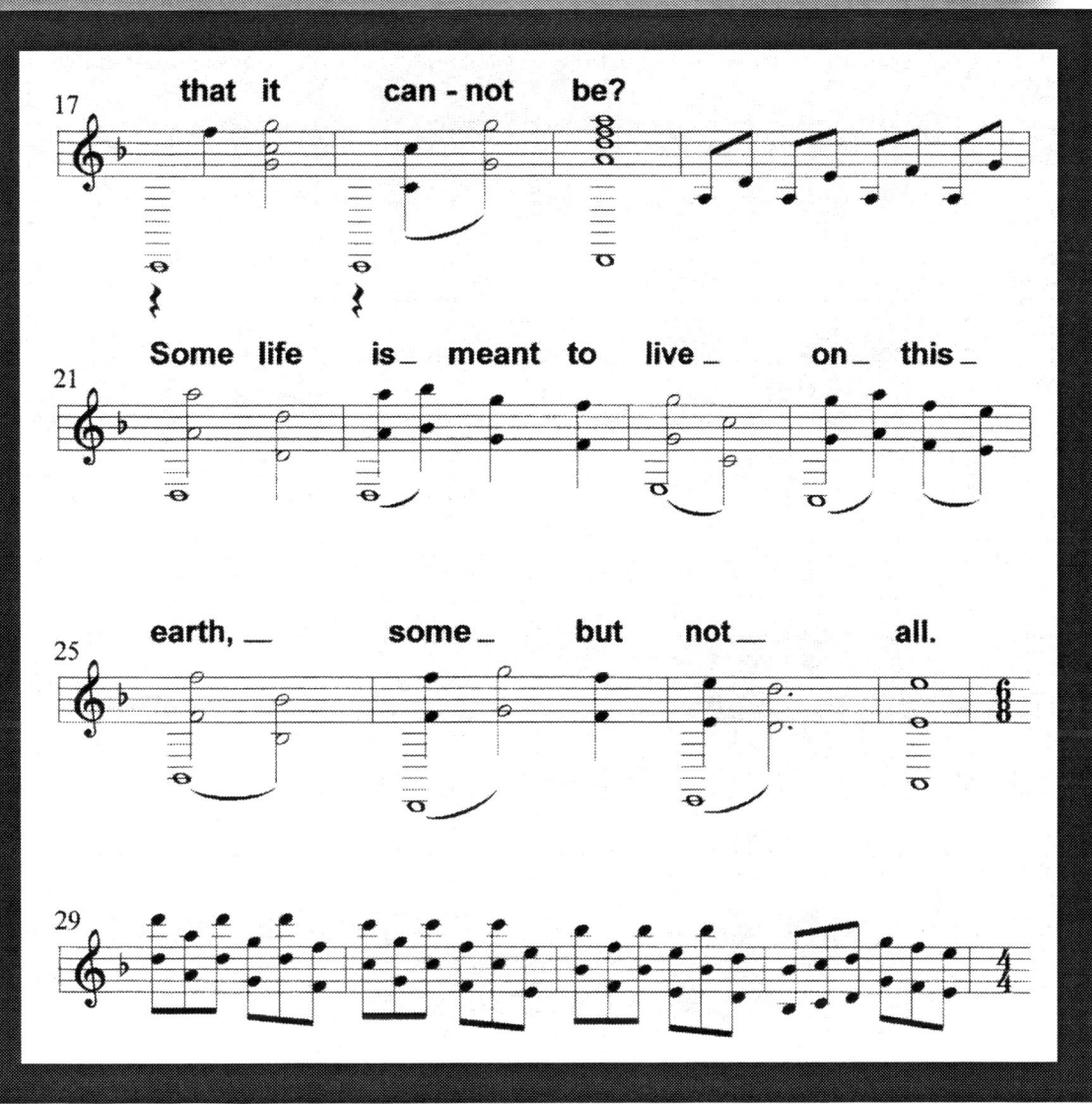

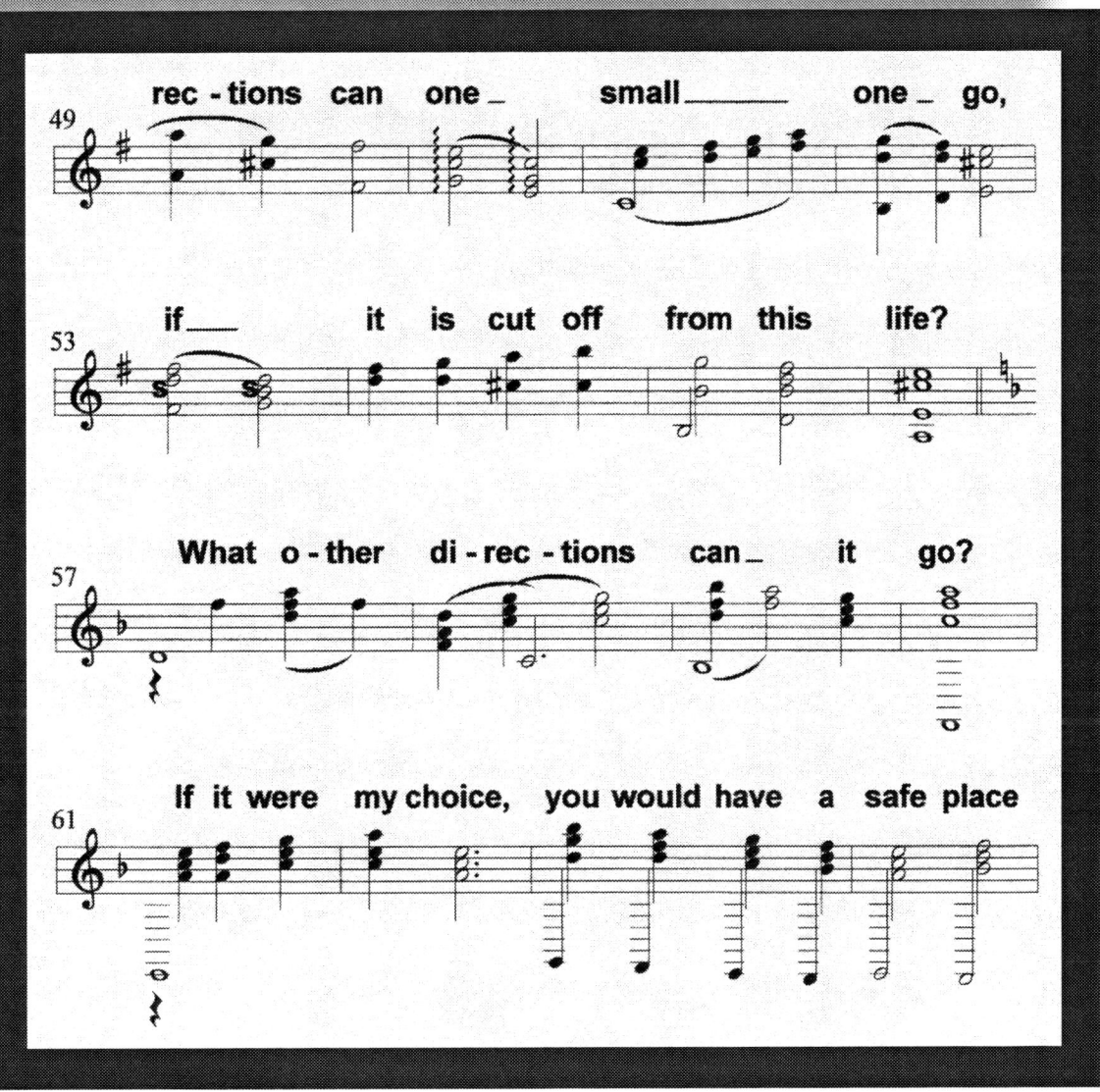

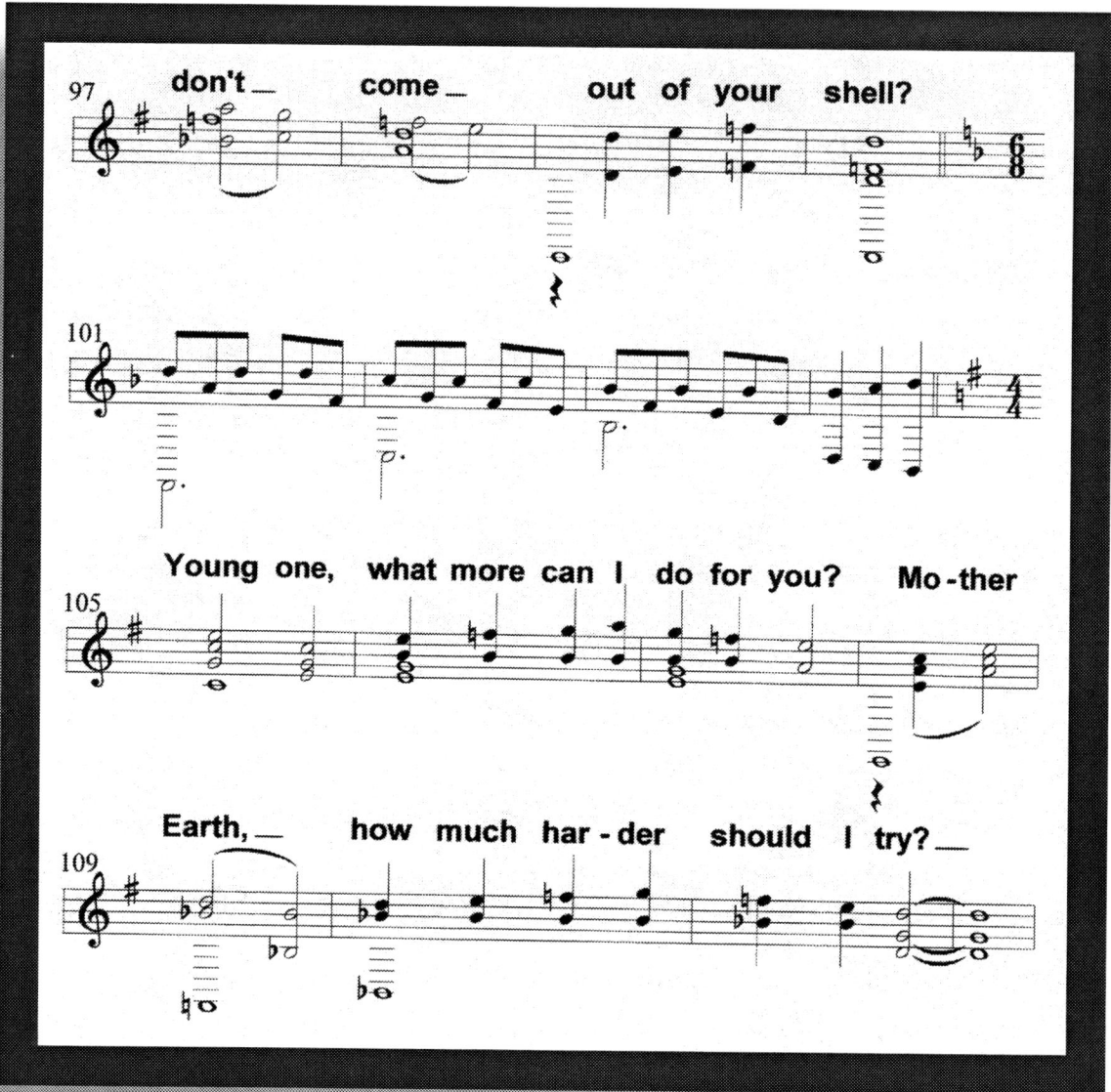

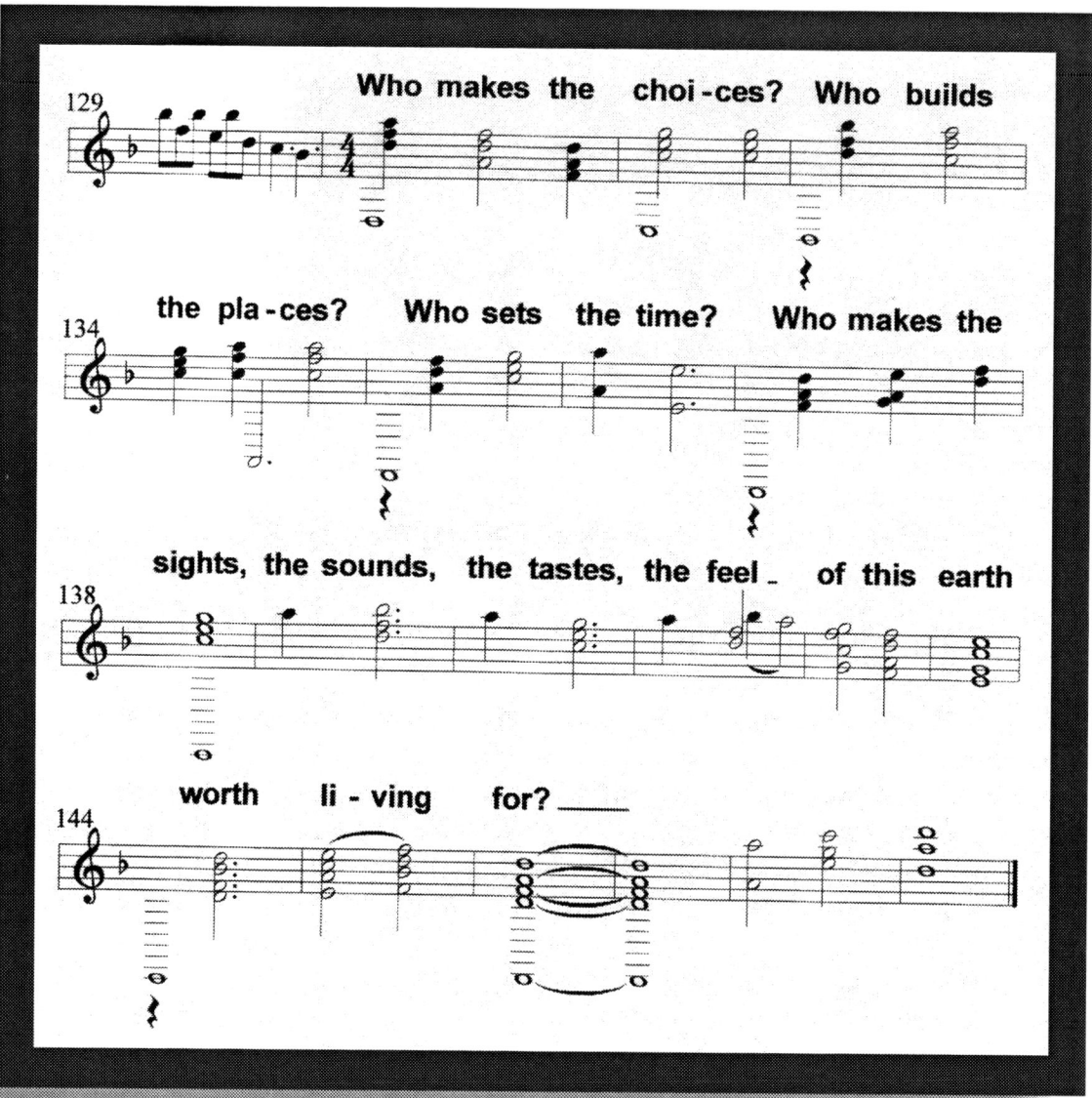

On the 18th morning—needing to stretch her wings and just get away—the hummingbird left the tree. Past the hills, across the valleys she flew aimlessly, struggling with her troubled thoughts.

Returning, she knew. She wanted to think differently as she hovered over the egg. But its warmth had disappeared.

All morning, she grieved motionless beside her nest.

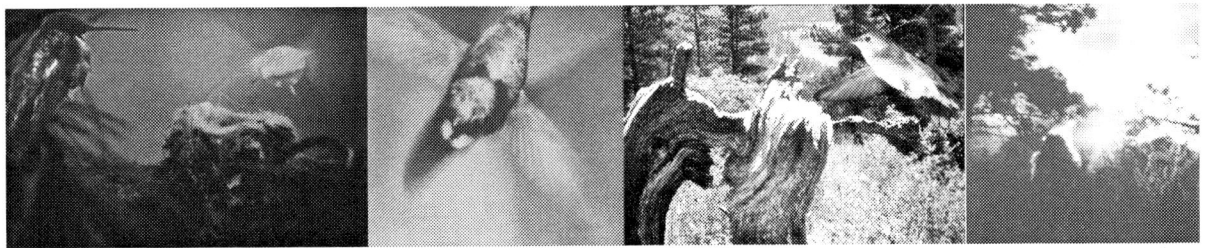

Toward afternoon, tall thunderheads billowed along the horizon. Wind burst from darkening skies.

Then, as suddenly as it had started, the wind stopped and a gentle rain began to fall.

Hearing the patter and trembling from it, the hummingbird abandoned her nest. Flittering blindly into the top branches past the twig that was her high post, she launched herself into the drizzle. Embracing the splatter, she crept upward toward the far end of the house, touching the rooftop, settling into the spray.

Raising her beak, fluffing her feathers, she closed her eyes and opened her heart.

Shivers ran through her from the moisture touching her hot skin. Shaking her head, she fluttered her wings and cast off toward the hills.

In the deep trees, it did not take long to feel the gentle murmur, a subtle musing, the intuitive spark.

Abiding

(Adapted from a 19th century hymn by Alexander Ewing)

The September morning was cool and breezy. The hummingbird did not want to leave her perch, finding her solace instead between the clothespins holding the rows of colorful garments to the clotheslines. Their fluttering reverberated with the same invisible movement dancing through her feathers. There was no life in the garments, yet their movement carried hints of it, creating many images in her head.

But how long must she remain to interpret them, how far must she carry her worn-out body? Waiting like she must, it sometimes felt as if she were a cloud of insects deciding whether or not to scatter across the open sky.

Each night grew cooler and each day the sun bore down. From the swaying hollyhocks, a few roses and honeysuckle vines, and the butterfly bushes still in bloom, she maintained enough energy to fly.

But those trips were growing shorter and could not last much longer. Often she waited on the rooftop for answers. The redness of the shingles and the sunsets taunted her, and visions of a returning light were more vivid than ever.

It was a quiet afternoon and the woman, in her final weeks of pregnancy, was poking through the hollyhocks, picking at the seed pods and touching the few remaining blooms, remembering the range of colors they had put out all summer. Her son and daughter joined her.

Their presence in the flowers seemed a curious thing for the hummingbird, watching from her post at the top branch of the tree. Suddenly the whole scene took on significant meaning. Could it be that these upright creatures also felt the same powers as she? Or shared the same spirit? Must they also, like her, pass through the same veil?

Sensing imperceptible possibilities build throughout her frame, she rose from her perch. From the tree, her flight upward and then toward the upright creatures was rather wobbly.

Clasping the white cloth on the boy's shoulder, the hummingbird waited. The girl gasped and the woman let go of the flower.

Slowly, the boy turned his head, and stared.

Immediately, the hummingbird knew. These upright creatures were intelligent; their attachment to nature was real.

The boy placed his forefinger against the hummingbird's breast. Without hesitation, she fluttered onto it. He glanced at his mother and sister, smiling wondrously. He held the hummingbird out to them, and they took turns stroking its head and back.

Attracted to the woman's pink sweater, the hummingbird fluttered to her hand. Immediately, a wave of calmness swept through the two—a hope and affection that all mothers know. The woman smiled as they shared the same light, the same tender truth.

Touch My Soul

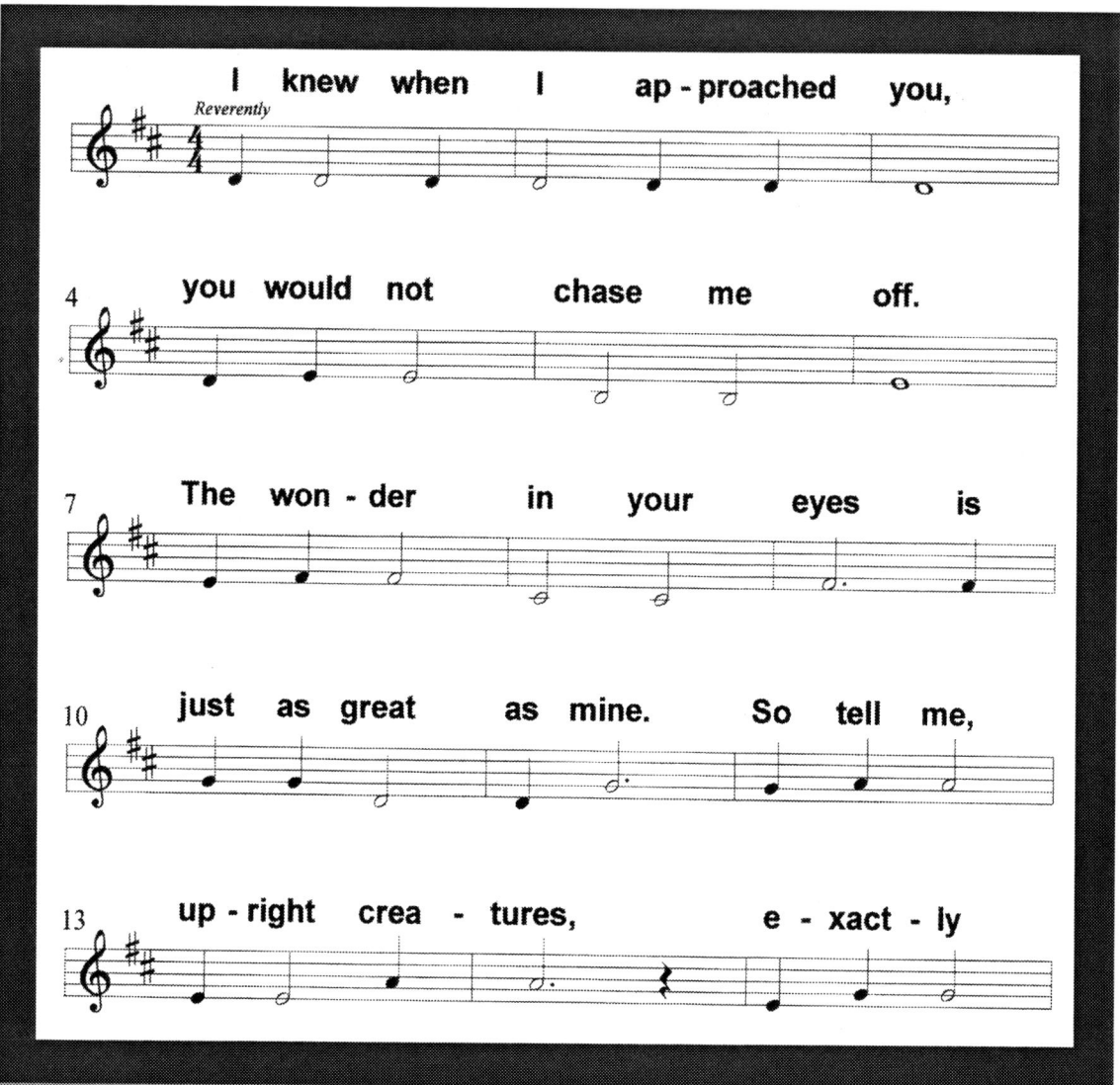

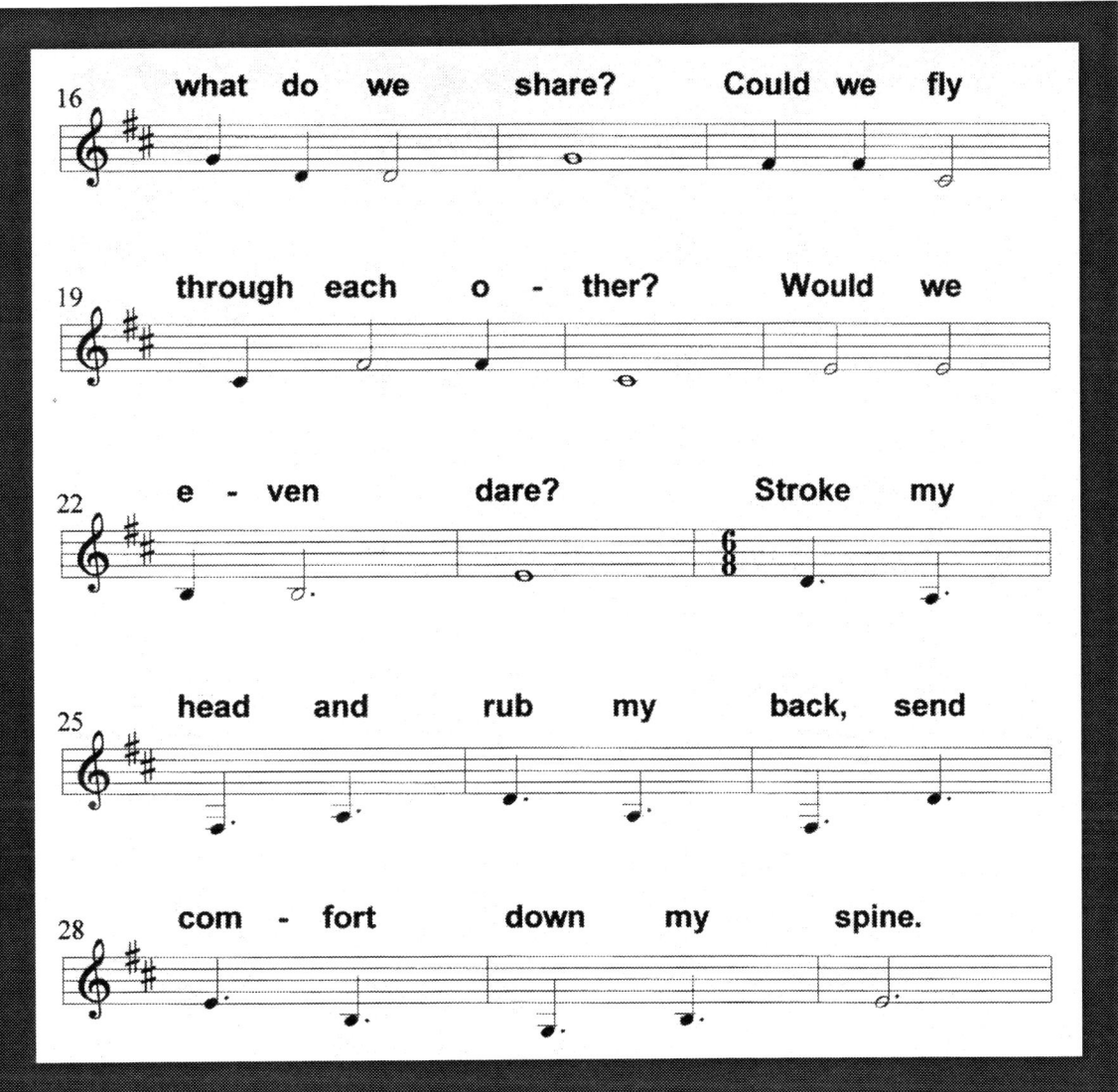

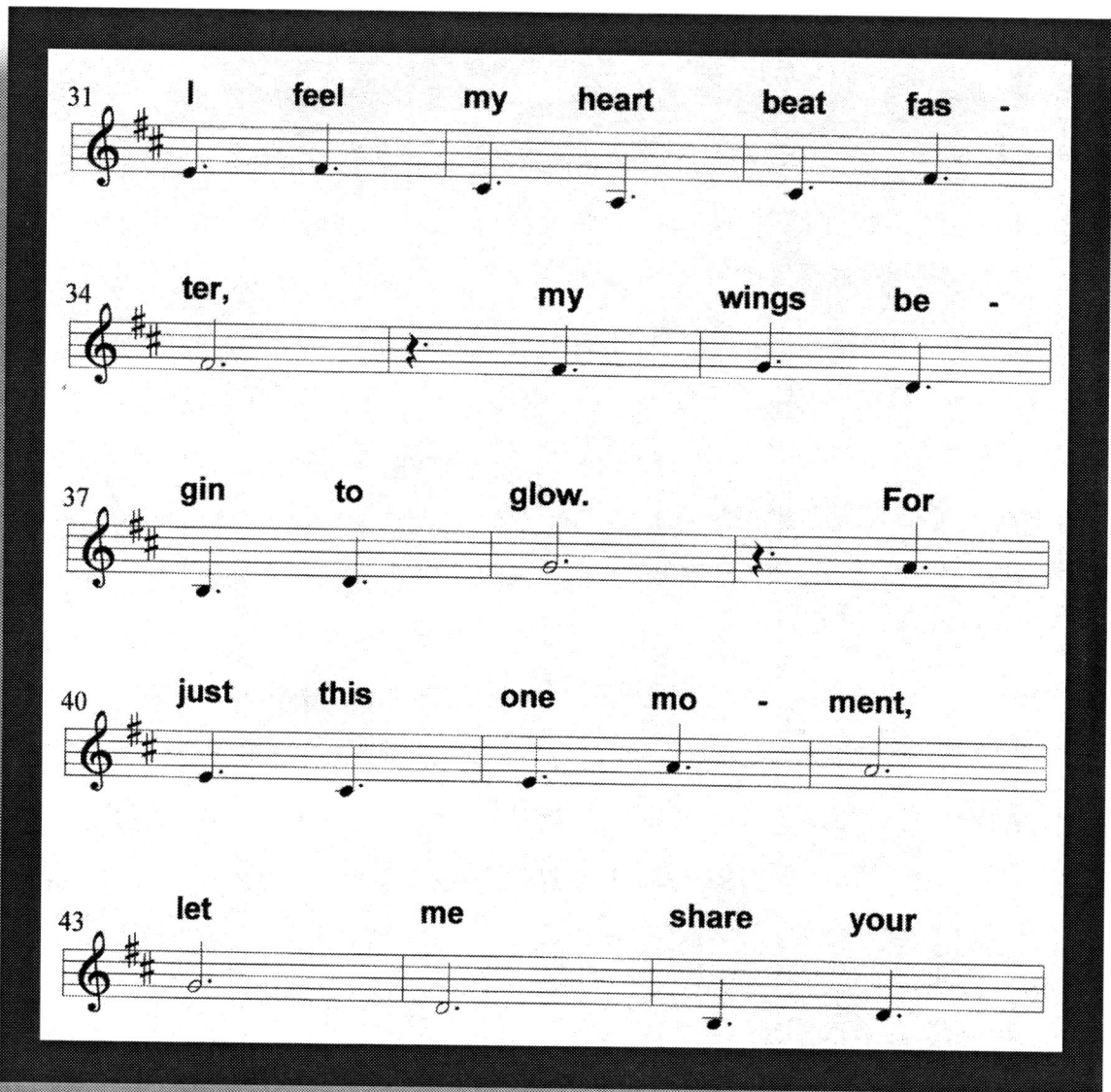

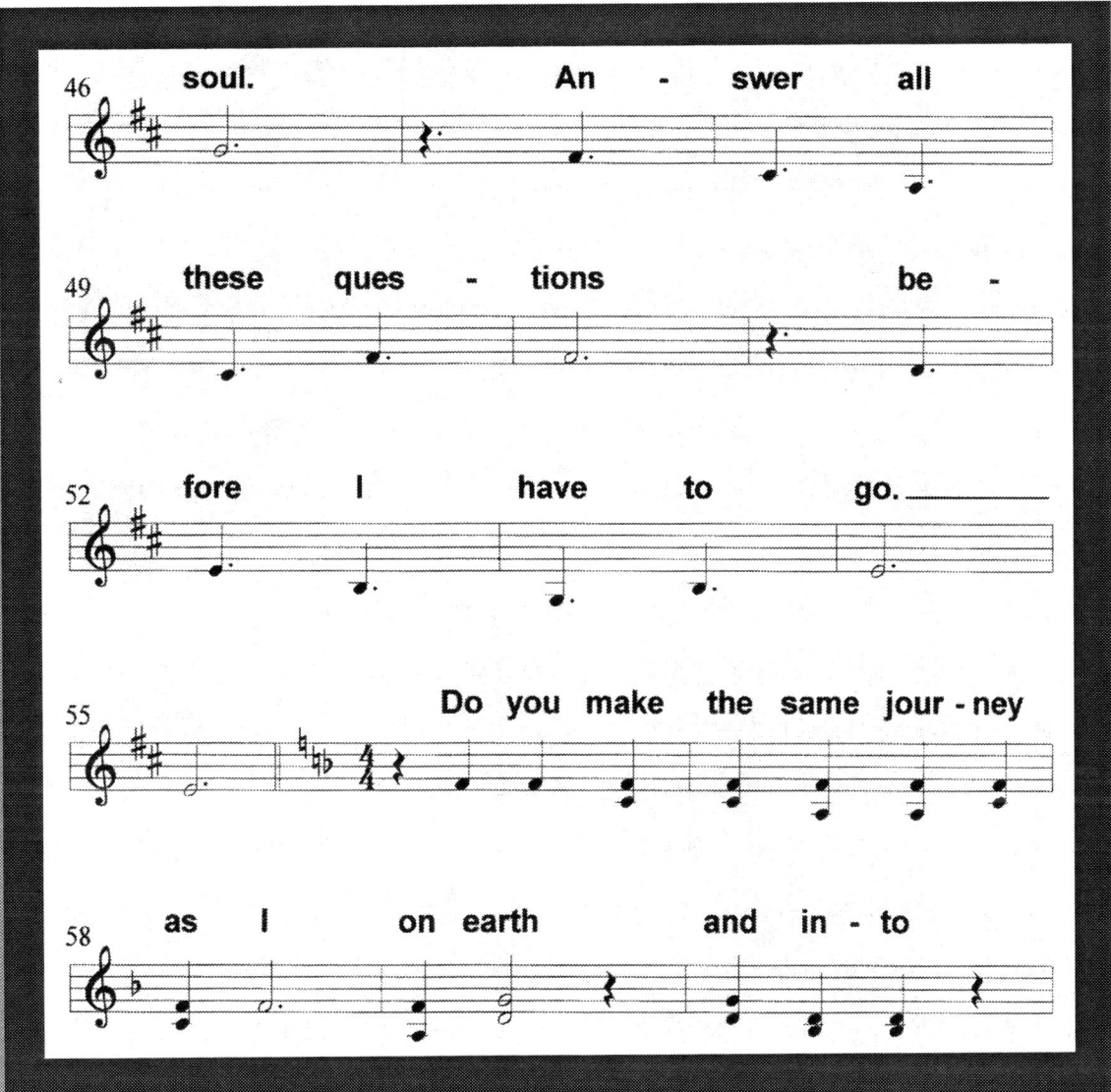

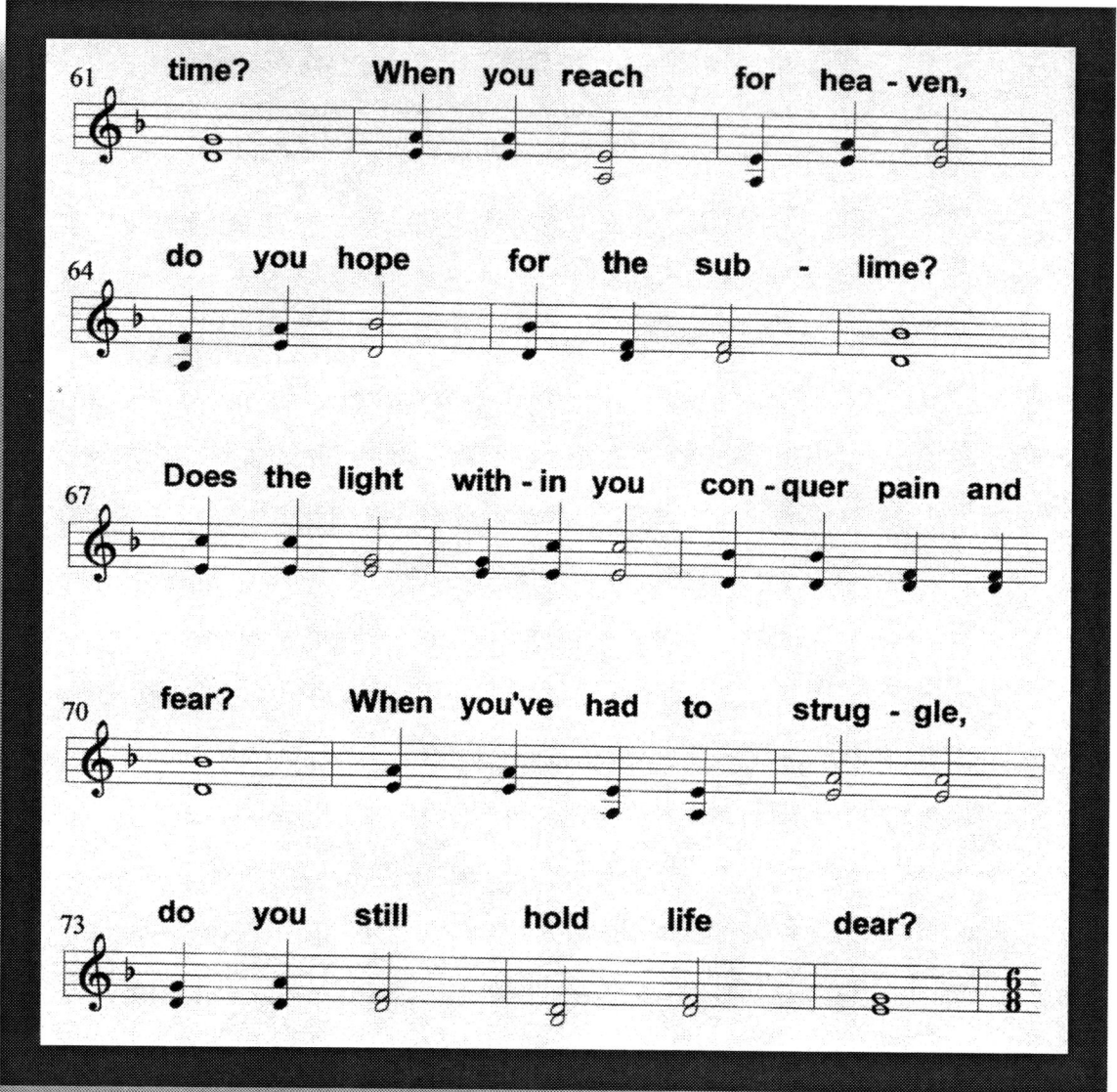

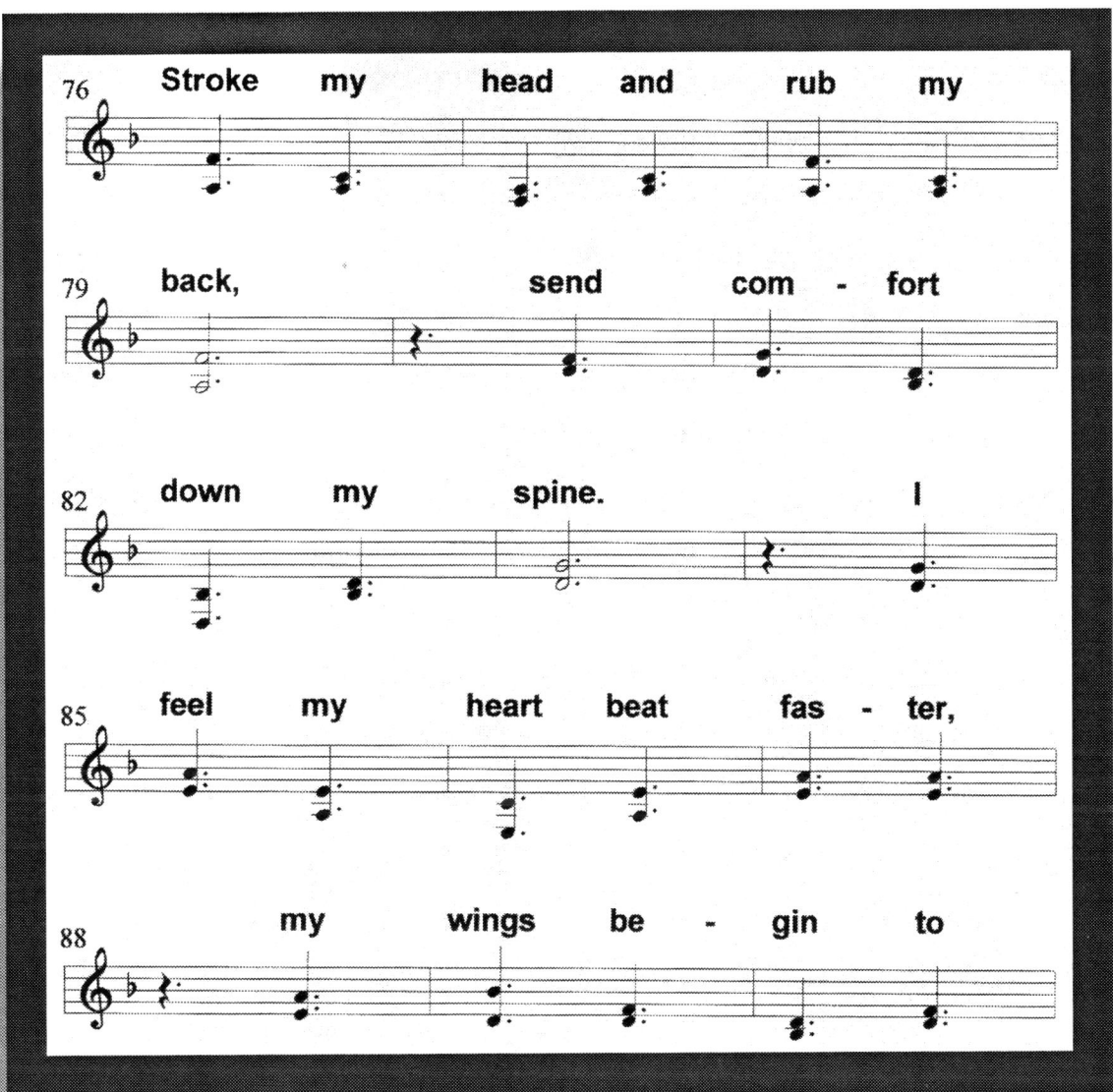

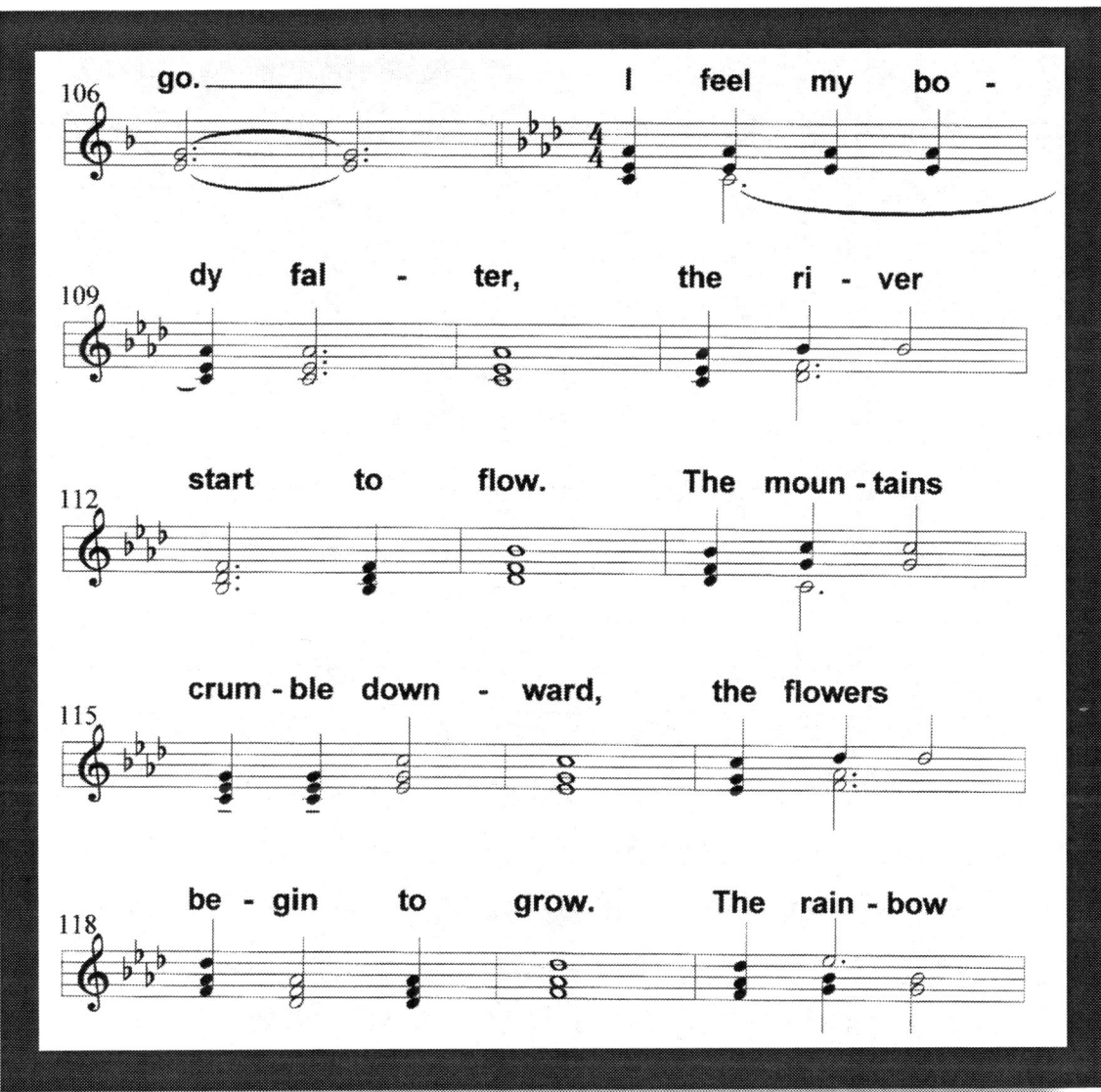

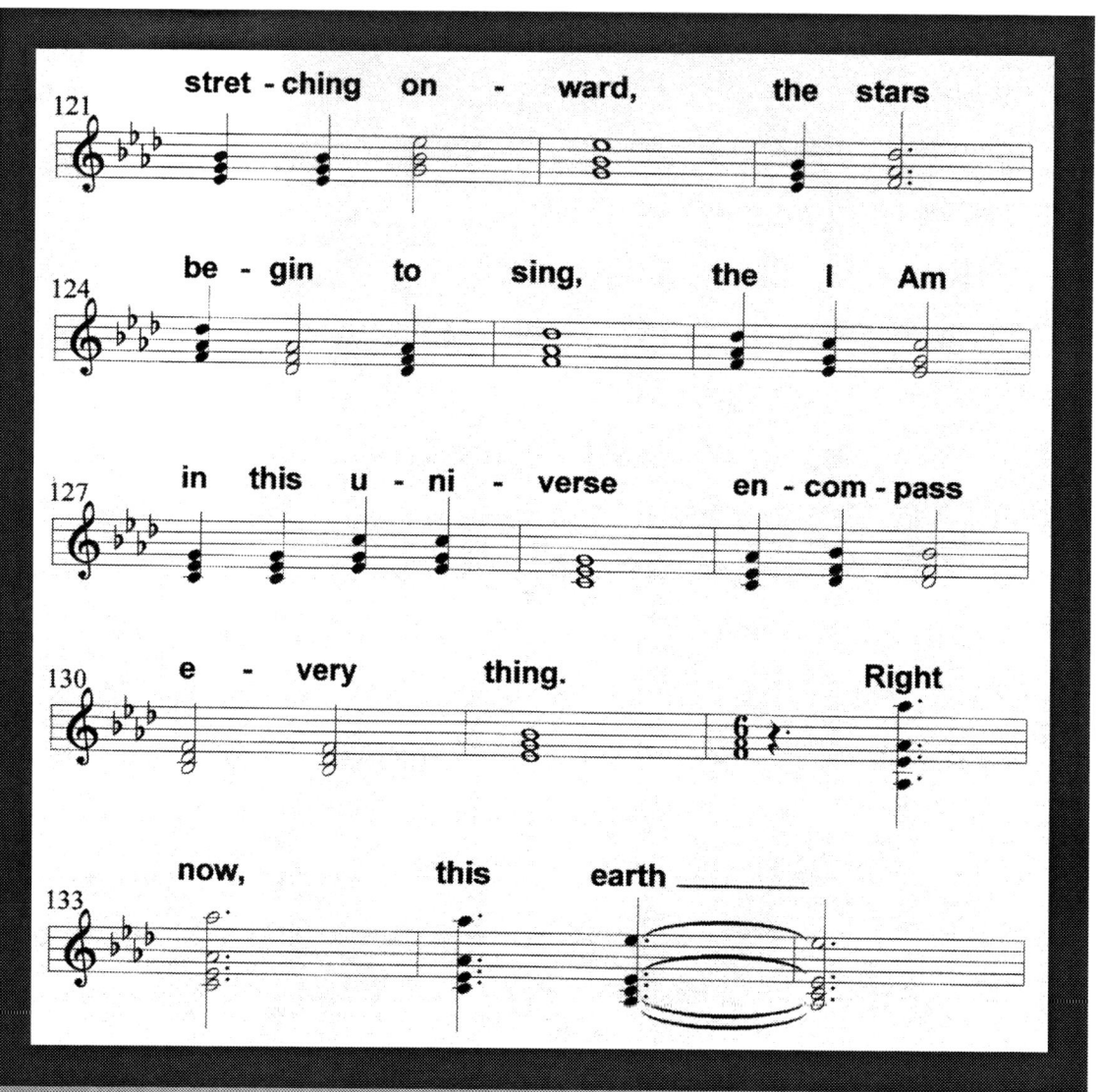

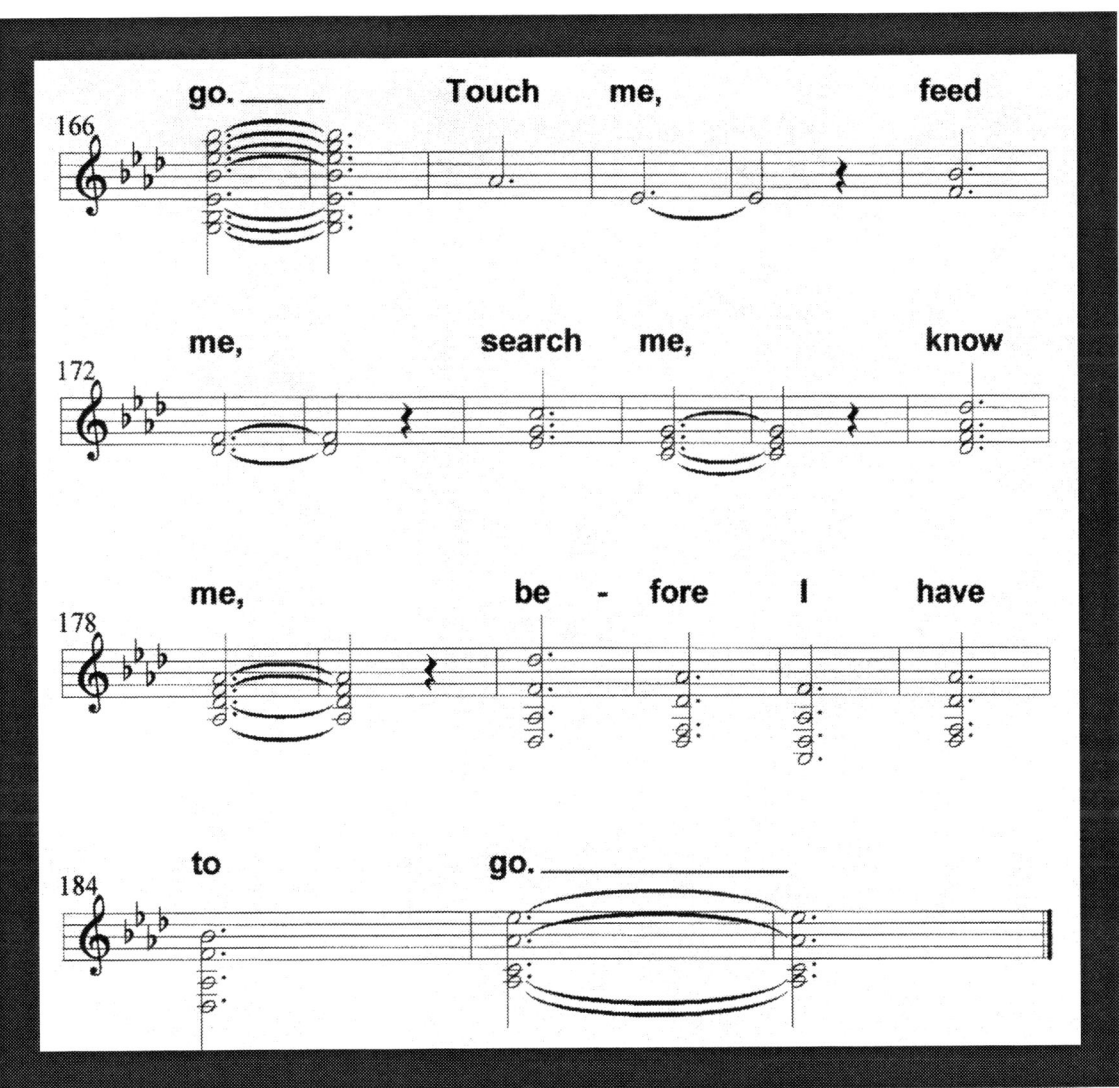

The woman stroked the bird's head and back. Her daughter reached up and did the same.

The boy picked a hollyhock bloom and held it close to the hummingbird's beak. To their awe, she reached in and sipped. Backing out, she cleared the nectar from the edges of her beak with her white tongue. Rubbing her beak against his finger, she wiped away some of the pollen grains.

Fifteen minutes passed. A slight breeze rustled through the hollyhocks and a cloud moved over the sun. The hummingbird stared upward and the woman and her children plainly saw an otherworldly look in its dark eyes.

Suddenly, the hummingbird whirred her wings. Slowly, struggling, she rose toward the house and planted herself against a shingle halfway up the roof.

Looking back, she watched the upright creatures staring at her, shading their eyes from the sun. She remained motionless and thought hard.

Mother, son, and daughter knew the hummingbird was trying to communicate something to them. Frustrated, the boy pressed his hands against his head. The mother pulled her children beside her and slowly ran her fingers through their hair.

The hummingbird struggled farther up the roof and turned her head. The three were blurry now. But their image still remained sharply etched in her thought.

Dwelling on the glimmer she had seen in the upright creatures' eyes, she scanned the sky and knew that, on this earth, they too were on a journey. Like her, they also labored. They had built the throne under her feet just as she had built hers, and now she clung to it as she had clung to hers. But, as with her own, try as she might, she could never pull it with her to the stars.

Launching herself toward the open sky, she disappeared from their sight.

Night descended like an orbed veil and the trees near her were cast in deep shadow.

Remembering her fluffy, bright-eyed young ones near their nests testing their wings, taking to the air, ready to explore masses of flowers swaying wavelike on the slopes in the gentle breeze, the hummingbird ruffled her feathers.

And she remembered the great trips southward, and the warm rains, the green hillsides, the abundant flowers and insects of the wintering grounds, and the season of molting and the growing of new feathers.

She remembered the moments she spent on herself, basking luxuriously in the sun, fluttering through a misty shower or along some dew-drenched leaf, and preening and oiling her feathers.

Slowly, the nictitating membranes slid over her eyes and her eyelids flickered shut.

And the shingles on the roof of the house glowed in the moonlight. And an image, one she had seen before in the mountains, flittered downward from the far reaches of space.

In whose Mind had this marvelous light been formed? Under whose Wings had it been blessed?

Quickly, the hummingbird opened her eyes. One more flight, she knew...and quickly she dropped from the tree and perched on the clothesline.

Above the house, a light appeared. She blinked and shivered and her claws tingled. Great joy clasped at her heart as the Master Hummingbird shimmered brightly.

Traveler

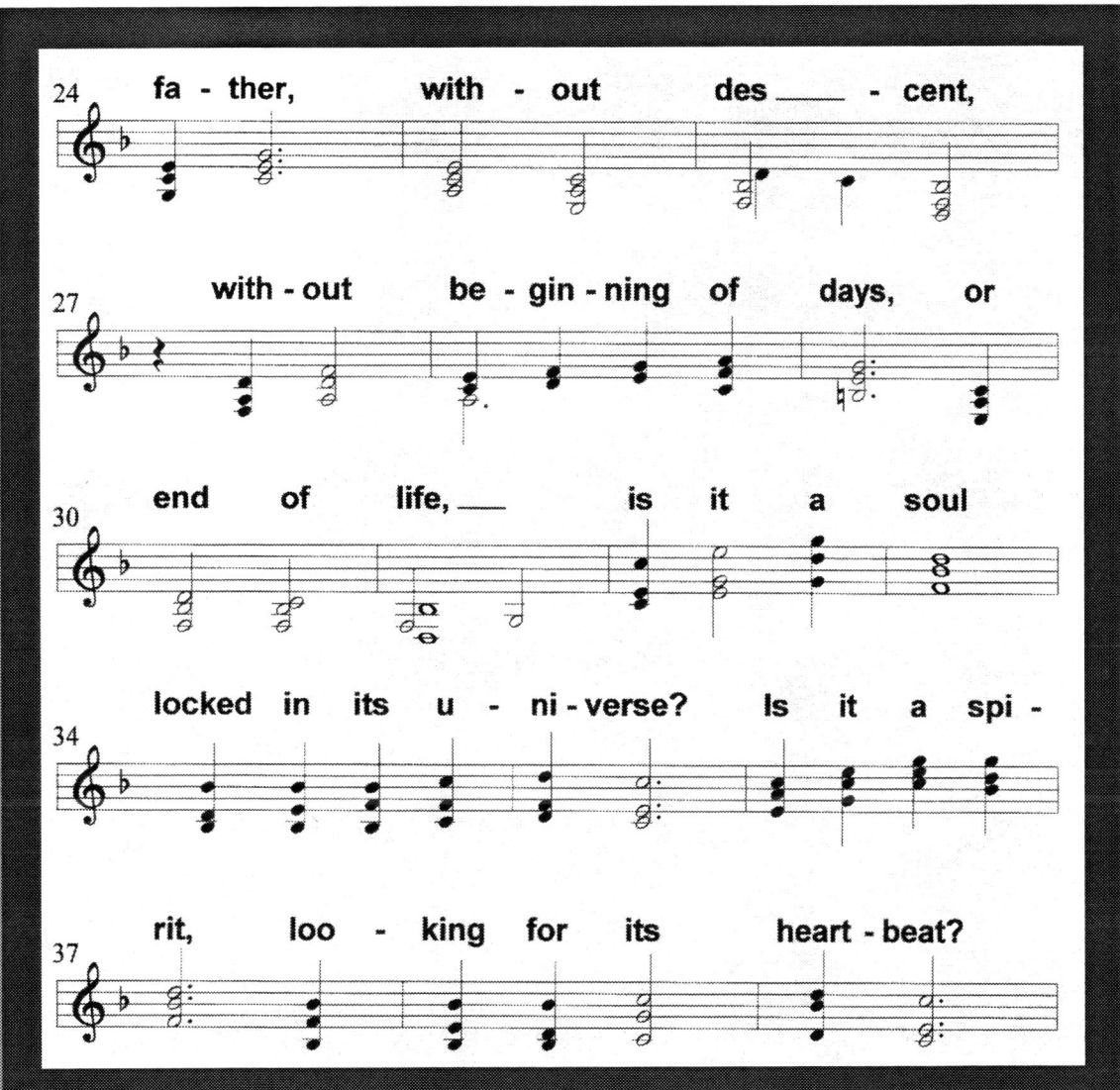

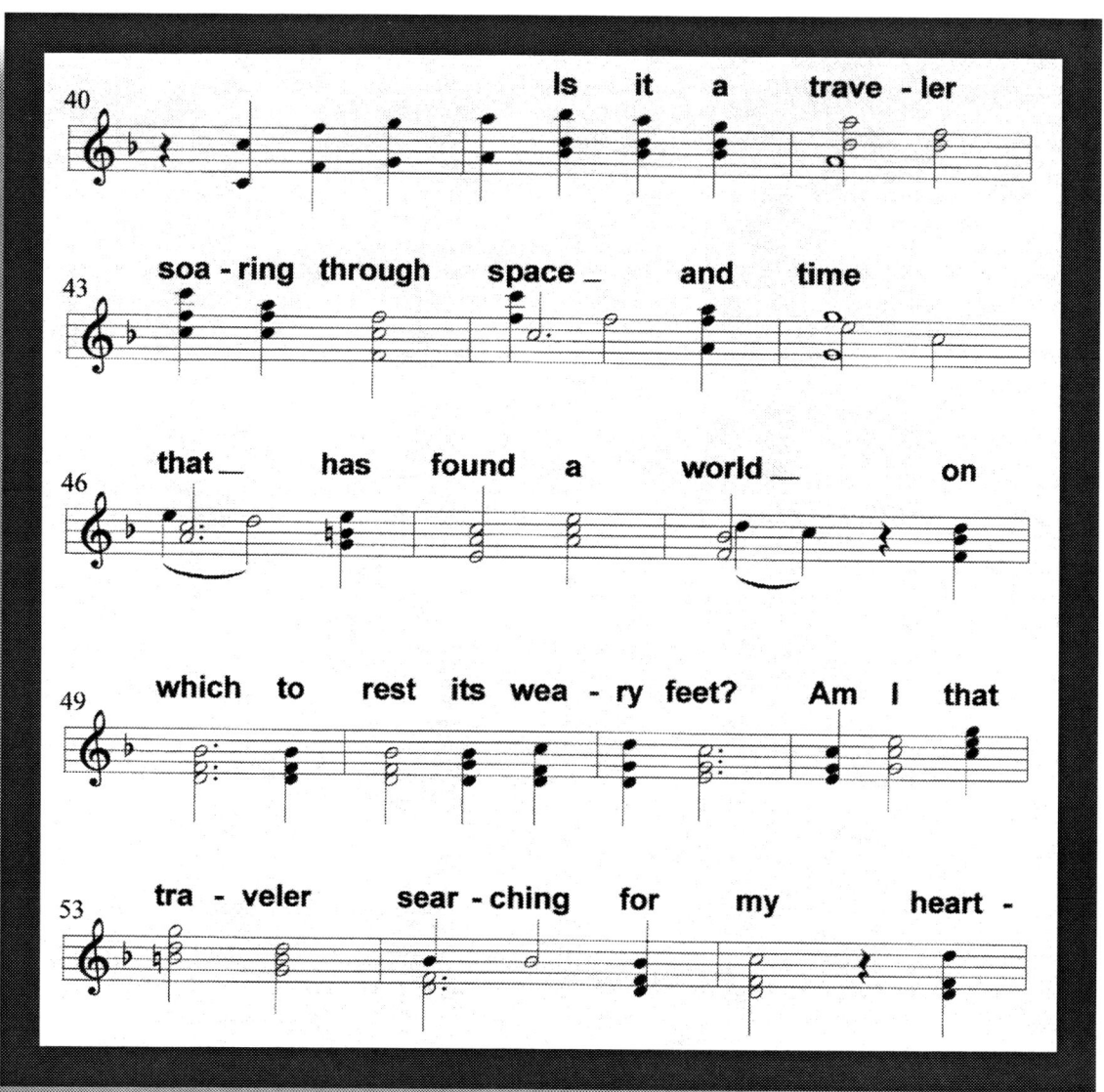

The old dog stepped off the porch and peered around the corner of the house. Slinking through the shadows toward the clothesline, he growled with trepidation.

Under the clothesline, he paced back and forth watching the light—the hair rising on his back. Unable to contain his excitement, he began to bark wildly.

There was a commotion in the house. The pup was barking. Familiar voices from the nearest bedroom window ordered both to hush up. Having heard the sharp words before, the old dog dropped to the ground and began to whine. Feeling currents of electricity seethe through him, he panted and drooled uncontrollably.

Above him, the hummingbird remained rigid as the scintillating light of the Master Hummingbird radiated infinite messages to her. She questioned, waited, and twitched her tail. Certainly, above her, there was a perpetual, heavenly flower opening. Certainly, the mass of insects she had earlier imagined herself to be was now ready to scatter across the open sky.

As the events and dreams of her earthly life once more swelled and rippled around her and against her in waves, flashing through her head, she wanted to reach up with her wings. Her heart strained as she felt her inner being pull outward and away and begin to rise. Releasing everything and yet remaining in its same shape, her spirit and soul spiraled upward...

And before her and within her and all around her was a crackling sound and the joyous flurry of a thousand hummingbird wings.

Overwhelmed, the tired dog felt the electricity diminish. Turning several times, he settled into the sticks and grit. Head cradled between front paws, tail swishing slowly back and forth, he watched the glow, shaped as a hummingbird, flutter and flicker and slowly diminish to a pinpoint of light.

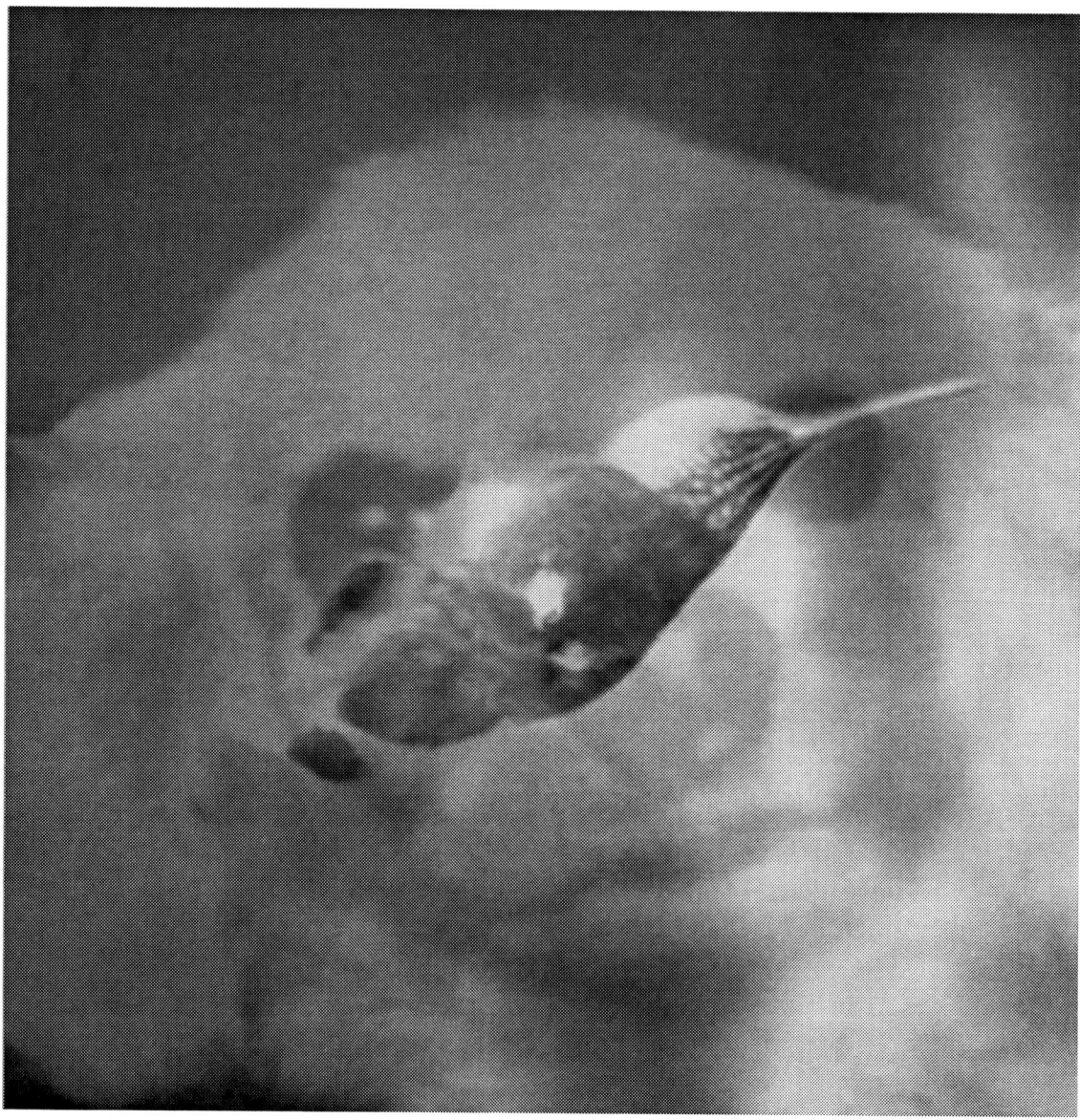

Epilogue

Tired because she had slept little the night before, the woman struggled to pull her husband's red shirt from the laundry basket. The pup was exploring under the clothesline and when the old dog stepped up and pressed his head against the woman's leg, she frowned impatiently and wanted to push him away. Hesitating, she saw the dark, plaintive look in his eyes.

He lifted his paw to her knee and started to whine. She rubbed his nose and scratched him behind the ears; of course he wanted her to sit down on the porch and lavish him with attention, just as her husband always did.

But there was laundry to hang up, baby clothes to mend, and garden vegetables to can and freeze. And when she was done with that, there would still be a million other things to do.

The old dog dropped his paw and trudged to the other end of the clothesline. There, he flopped his bone-weary body into the sticks and grit.

Yes, there was laundry to hang up, baby clothes to mend, and garden vegetables to can and freeze. Pinning her husband's shirt, the woman glanced down the line toward the family pets.

She froze, sadness creasing her brow. The pup was on its hind legs, looking up. The old dog once again began to whine.

"Holy hummingbird!" the woman whispered.

The old dog stood up, slowly swaying his tail.

Stepping past the basket, the flowers and up to the dogs, the woman held out her hand and the old one ardently licked it. Eyes misting, she bared her heart to what hung upside down before her on the clothesline.

"Poor, wonderful, beautiful little bird," she muttered. "Bless your iridescent soul."

What remained behind its closed eyes? Under its spotted throat and the russet and gray ruffled feathers? In its green iridescence? Wanting to lift the small bundle upright so she could stroke its head and back one more time, she touched the bird's beak.

A tingle seethed through her finger. Drawing away, she suddenly felt as if she were standing on the edge of a cliff, her melancholy twinged by a breeze.

Puzzled and excited, she touched the bird again.

This time, something more powerful surged through her, greater than any emotion. Eyes wide, she gasped, stepped back, looked down and quickly clasped her hands over her belly as it began to flutter wildly—more than it had ever fluttered before.

What was it causing her unborn one to kick and butt and poke so hard?

Why was her baby leaping with joy?

What You May or May Not Know About Hummingbirds

Approximately 400 varieties of hummingbirds exist in the Western Hemisphere. Twenty varieties live in or migrate to the United States during the summer months. Broadtails winter in the mountains of Mexico and Guatemala; during spring and early summer, they fly into New Mexico, Arizona, and range all the way to Montana and Idaho. Following the supply of flowers and insects, they breed at elevations between 4,000 and 12,700 feet. Rufouses spend their summers as far north as southern Alaska.

Hummingbirds are considered living jewels of the animal world. Their feathers contain layers of platelets filled with tiny air bubbles that partially reflect light, resulting in brilliant reds, greens, purples, and blues. When diving past the females during courtship, the males spread their throat patches, or gorgets, to fully advertise their nuptial intent.

Feisty and fearless, hummingbirds arch and dive through the air at speeds up to 45 miles per hour. Hovering effortlessly, they hold their bodies nearly upright while flapping horizontally in a shallow figure eight. To fly backwards, they reach back and scoop air like a swimmer doing the backstroke. If they want to fly upside down, they simply spread their tails and somersault backwards.

To move air up and down and back and forth more than 50 times a second (up to 200 times a second during courtship flight), a hummingbird has chest muscles making up 30% of its weight. Heart pumping at 1,200 beats per minute, a hummingbird requires approximately 155,000 calories a day. You or I would have to eat 370 pounds of boiled potatoes or 285 pounds of ground beef to produce that energy! Weighing in at three grams—as much as a penny—a hummingbird eats half its weight in sugar every 24 hours.

Males and females often establish separate territories, and carefully adjust the size to their feeding demands. When food becomes scarce, they may go into a night-time torpor to preserve energy, although incubating females must stay conscious and metabolically active to keep their eggs warm through cool nights.

A female hummingbird normally lays two eggs, the size of peas. Incubation lasts approximately 17 days. Unlike some birds, the young ones are helpless when they hatch, but are ready to test their wings and leave the nest at about three weeks.

Except when gathering around a hummingbird feeder, hummingbirds usually travel alone. When seasons change, individuals can be seen and heard buzzing overhead toward the next supply of food. The ideal mixture for a hummingbird feeder is one part sugar to five parts boiled water.

Note: M. L Stevens photographed the hummingbirds in Iridescent Soul on Lookout Mountain west of Denver, Colorado.

As a musician or a leader of a choir, band, or theater group, do you think you could make the music of Iridescent Soul soar and reverberate? Would one or two of these songs be inspirational if performed in your church? If you aspire musically, you are invited to perform individual songs or record the whole set. Professional and amateur musicians' CDs and other recordings of the work will be considered for sale on the author's official website:

www.soultrails.com .